THE BOY ALLIES WITH

THE COSSACKS

CLAIR W. HAYES

THE BOY ALLIES WITH THE COSSACKS

CHAPTER I

FLYING

"What's that below, Hal?"

The speaker was Chester Crawford, an American lad of some 16 years.

Hal Paine allowed his eyes to turn from the steering wheel and glanced over the side of the flying aëroplane.

"I don't see anything," he replied, after a careful scrutiny below.

"Neither do I, now," said Chester, straining his eyes.

At this moment the third occupant of the machine made his presence known.

"Woof! Woof!" he exclaimed.

The third speaker was Marquis, a dog.

"Woof! Woof!" he barked again.

Hal, with a quick move, slackened the speed of the aëroplane, and let it glide gently closer to the earth.

"Must be something wrong," he confided to Chester, "or Marquis wouldn't be barking like that."

Both lads peered into the darkness that engulfed them on all sides. As far as the eye could penetrate there was nothing but blackness, solid, intense.

"Let's go a little lower, Hal," whispered Chester.

Under Hal's firm hand the aëroplane came down gently, until at last it was soaring close to the treetops. And now, suddenly, both lads made out the cause of Marquis's uneasiness.

Beneath them were thousands upon thousands of armed men. To the north, to the south, and to the east and west the dense mass of humanity

2

stretched out. Hal and Chester, flying close to the earth, at last could make out moving forms below them.

Suddenly it became light. Not broad daylight, but the darkness gave way enough for the lads to distinguish what lay below them. The dawn of another day was breaking.

At the same instant that the lads made out the huge mass of humanity upon the ground their presence in the air was discovered. There came the sound of a single shot and the whiz of a bullet, as it sped close to Hal's ear.

With a quick movement the lad sent the plane soaring high in the air once more. So sudden was the movement that Chester, caught unprepared, lost his balance, and saved himself from tumbling to the ground only by clutching the side of the machine. Marquis also had a narrow escape from being thrown out. He let out a loud yelp of fear, as he was thrown violently against Chester. The lad threw out a hand and grabbed him by the scruff of the neck, just as it seemed he would plunge to certain destruction.

"Say!" he called to Hal, when he finally regained his breath and his head. "What's the matter with you? You almost dumped us both out."

"Did I?" replied Hal briefly. "Well, as long as you didn't fall it's all right. We had to come up suddenly, or the chances were we would have gone down suddenly. But it's my fault. I should have given you warning. Are you hurt?"

"No," replied Chester.

"I'll be careful next time," said Hal. "You'll have to forgive me this once."

"Say no more about it," answered Chester. "But what was the cause of this sudden rise?"

"Cause!" repeated Hal in astonishment. "You don't mean to tell me you don't know the cause? Didn't you hear that shot?"

"Yes, I heard it. But how do you know whether it was fired by friend or foe?"

"I can't see as that would make any difference if it happened to hit us. However, I'm morally certain they were Germans."

"Well, maybe they were. What are we going to do now?"

3

"We'll stay up here until we are absolutely certain we have passed over the German lines. Then we'll come down."

The machine was high in the air now, and, peering intently over the side, as he did, Chester was unable to make out anything below in the early morning light.

But in the rear, soaring high in the air, although neither lad realized it, a new danger threatened. When the presence of the boys' plane had been discovered, a German craft had immediately risen, and was now in pursuit.

Glancing over his shoulder, Chester was the first to discover that they were followed. At the same moment that he perceived the pursuing machine there came a shot from the enemy.

There was no need for Chester to cry out to Hal. The sound of the shot told the latter of their danger, and he immediately threw the speed lever over as far as it would go.

The machine bounded forward.

But the pursuer also came on faster than before; and, while it was apparent that he was not lessening the distance between the two craft, he nevertheless was still in range, and his rifle continued to crack. However, neither the machine nor its three occupants were struck.

Chester took a snap shot at the other craft with his revolver, but the bullet fell short. While the enemy could pepper them at will with his rifle, a bullet from the lad's revolver could not reach him.

Hal heard the sound of Chester's revolver, and called out:

"Did you hit him?"

"No!" Chester shouted back, "he's too far behind. But he'll get us in a minute if we don't do something." To himself he added: "If I only had a rifle!"

"You be ready with your revolver," Hal called to his friend, "and I'll soon fix that. It's our only chance."

Abruptly he slackened the speed of the machine, and swiftly the enemy came on. So suddenly had Hal acted that the man at the wheel of the pursuing machine could not act promptly enough, and was within range of Chester's revolver before he could slow down.

As the first machine righted after its abrupt halt, Chester took deliberate aim and fired, even at the moment that a bullet passed close to his head.

There was a yell from the pursuing machine. A man leaped suddenly to his feet, shaking the frail craft violently as he did so, waved his arms once, twice, and toppled into space.

"I got one of 'em," Chester shouted to Hal, and his lips shut grimly.

"Good for you!" Hal shouted back.

Even Marquis realized that it was time to be pleased, and he sent up a sharp bark of joy. His canine intelligence told him that something that threatened had been overcome.

But the man at the wheel of the German aëroplane, now that he was alone, was not minded to give up the chase. The machine darted at the boys' craft suddenly, and, but for the fact that Hal at that very moment happened to glance over his shoulder, the sharp-pointed prow of the German craft would have cut them down.

With a sudden twist of the wheel, however, Hal sent the machine out of the path of the German, and, as the enemy sped by, Chester took a snap shot with his revolver.

Evidently he missed, for the German checked his plane and returned to the attack.

"So," said Hal to himself, "two can play at that game."

Once more he avoided the German rush; and then, wheeling his own craft at the moment the German sped by, he dashed in pursuit. The enemy, doing the work of two men, did not perceive this change in tactics by his foes, and, even as he slowed down to turn and make another attack, the point of the lad's machine plowed into him.

There was a ripping, tearing sound; the German plane wavered and started to fall as the craft in which the boys were flying dashed by. But, by a superhuman effort, the German succeeded in righting his craft.

Then, holding the wheel steady with one hand, he calmly produced a revolver and took deliberate aim at Hal.

5

There was a sharp crack, followed immediately by another, but Hal was unharmed.

Realizing the German's purpose, Chester's weapon had spoken a second before that of the enemy. The lad had not had time to take careful aim, but the bullet sped true, striking the German squarely in the forehead, even at the moment his finger pressed the trigger of his own revolver.

Chester saw the man throw up his hands and fall backward. The German plane, now without a hand to keep it steady, rocked crazily for several moments, then turned turtle and went tumbling over and over toward the ground.

"Did you get him, Chester?" asked Hal, who had not turned his head, and therefore had not perceived his own danger.

"Yes, I got him," replied Chester simply.

"Good!" returned Hal. "And the machine?"

"Gone!"

The lads now paused to take stock of their own damage, if any. There was none. Not a German bullet had so much as struck the machine.

"They are not very good marksmen, are they?" said Hal, with a slight grin.

"Doesn't look that way," returned Chester. "However, maybe those fellows are not the best specimens."

"Maybe not," replied Hal.

"What next?" asked Chester, after a slight pause.

"Guess we might as well go on," replied Hal. "There may be some more of those German machines flying after us, so I guess it behooves us to get away from here as soon as possible."

"I guess you are right," Chester acquiesced.

Once more the aëroplane straightened itself out on its course and, flying high–absolutely hidden from the ground by a dense mass of black clouds that seemed to spring up as if by magic–sped on.

Hal, with firm hands on the wheel, kept his gaze directly ahead. Chester settled himself comfortably in his seat again, and Marquis, after sniffing about for several moments, finally composed himself to sleep.

In spite of the fact that he was flying far above ground, the dog had not shown a sign of nervousness or fright. Evidently he had no fear. Possibly through his head flashed the thought that if these young boys who were caring for him had saved him once, it was no more than they would do again.

CHAPTER II

BEYOND THE ENEMY

Hal Paine and Chester Crawford, two young American lads, had already seen much active service in the great European war of 1914, the greatest war of all history.

With Hal's mother they had been in the capital of Germany when the conflagration broke out. In making their way from Berlin they had been separated from Mrs. Paine and, thrown upon their resources, it became necessary for them to make their way out of Germany alone, or else to stay in Berlin for an indefinite time. The boys elected to leave.

With Major Raoul Derevaux, a French Officer, then a captain, and Captain Harry Anderson, an Englishman, they had finally succeeded in making their way into the Belgian lines. They had witnessed the heroic defense of the Belgians at Liège, and had themselves taken part in the battle. Having accomplished several missions successfully, they had come to be looked upon with the greatest respect by the Belgian commander.

At Louvain Hal was wounded, and Chester had him conveyed to Brussels. Here the lads again fell in with Captain Anderson, and, through the good offices of the latter, eventually found themselves attached to the British forces on the continent. They had gained favor in the eyes of Sir John French, the British Field Marshal in command of the British troops, and had successfully accomplished several difficult missions.

Taken prisoners by the Germans, they had been saved from death at the hands of a firing squad by the Emperor of Germany himself, and had finally been taken back to Berlin.

In the streets of the German capital, one day, a message had been put into their hands by an English prisoner, who declared that its delivery to the Grand Duke Nicholas, commander of the hosts of the Czar of Russia, was a matter of much moment.

Displaying great resourcefulness and bravery, the lads had succeeded in escaping from Berlin in an aëroplane, as narrated in "The Boy Allies on the Firing Line," the same in which, at the opening of this story, we find them flying swiftly eastward.

Crack revolver shots, and having skill in the use of the sword and with their fists, the boys had fought themselves out of many ticklish situations. And now, free again, they were making all speed to deliver the message from the combined leaders of two countries to Grand Duke Nicholas, a message that would mean closer coöperation between the Russians in the east and the British and French forces in the west.

The Russian campaign so far could hardly be called a success. True, the first German advance into Poland, with Warsaw as its object, had been checked, and the invader had been driven back; but the mighty legions of the Czar of all the Russias could not be mobilized with the swiftness of the Kaiser's troops; and, when mobilized, could not be transported to the front with the same dispatch.

Reënforced after their first defeat in Poland, the Germans had begun a new drive into the heart of Poland. Day after day they drew nearer and nearer to the little capital, Warsaw–the Russians retreating before them.

But now, within two days' march of Warsaw, the Russians held steadily, and, try as he might, the German commander could not break through this line of steel. Grand Duke Nicholas, commander-in-chief of the Russian armies–who at first had been with the southern army opposing the Austrians and advancing upon Cracow, in Galicia–had hurried north, to take personal command in Poland.

His presence had instilled new vigor into the Russian troops, and, after several days of defensive action, the Russian troops had at last resumed the offensive.

It was toward this mighty army that the aëroplane that had borne the boys through the heart of the enemy was now flying swiftly.

"Seems to me," said Hal, "that by this time we must have passed the German lines. I guess we might as well go down a bit and have a look around."

Accordingly the machine glided nearer the earth. The day was dark and foggy, and at first the lads could discern nothing below but a great blur.

They drew closer.

At that moment there came a shot from below. Hal instinctively threw over the lever in an effort to take the craft out of harm's way.

But the machine did not respond to his touch.

9

"Great Scott!" he cried. "That one bullet must have put us out of commission. We'll have to go down, or be shot to pieces up here."

Gently the little craft glided toward the earth; and now the boys could make out the objects below.

On all sides, stretching out as far as the eye could see, was a mighty mass of moving men.

"Germans?" asked Chester anxiously.

"We'll soon see," replied Hal briefly.

It was apparent now that those below, realizing that the aircraft was falling, would not fire at it again. With upturned eyes thousands of men watched the flight of the little plane, as it soared down among them.

Hal looked closely at the men, as the machine drew near the ground, and then exclaimed:

"No, they are not Germans; Russians, that's what they are."

Chester raised a feeble cheer.

"Hurrah!" he shouted.

Marquis, aroused by the sound of the lad's voices, arose and stretched. Even he seemed pleased.

And now the aëroplane bumped the ground, and the lads stepped out to see a long line of rifle barrels confronting them.

The lads threw up their hands instantly, but Marquis's back bristled and he growled threateningly.

"Keep quiet!" Chester commanded, and the dog grew still. An officer approached the lads.

"What do you here?" he demanded, in some language the lads could not understand.

The lads shook their heads, and the officer tried again, this time in German.

"What do you here?" he demanded.

As briefly as possible, Hal, acting as spokesman, explained. The officer's incredulous gaze grew more so as the lad went on with his story. When the lad had finished, he said simply:

"I don't believe you!"

Hal was angry in a second. He took a step toward the officer.

"What do you mean by that?" he demanded.

The officer stood his ground.

"Just what I say," he replied. "I don't believe you. The tale you tell is impossible."

Chester stepped into the breach. He took Hal by the arm.

"Of course such a tale is hard to believe," he said. "But, nevertheless, it is true. We carry an important message for the Grand Duke."

"Well," said the officer, "I don't think you will see him. He is too busy to give up his time to listen to such a tale as yours."

But at this moment a second officer, apparently the other's superior, approached. To him, upon request, Hal repeated his story. This officer also looked incredulous, but the result was different.

"You tell a very strange story," he said, "but it is not for me to pass upon its veracity. You shall be given an audience with the Grand Duke; but, mark me well, if it is found that you have been lying–that you have nothing of importance, it will go hard with you."

"We have no fear of that, sir," said Chester briefly.

"All right, then. Follow me."

The lads did as ordered, Marquis trailing along after them. Through thousands of rapidly-moving men the lads followed the officer, and at last, after more than an hour's walk, came to a stop, upon command, in front of a large, bewhiskered man, of imposing military stature.

"This," said the officer who had conducted them, "is Grand Duke Nicholas."

The officer looked down on them.

11

"What is it?" he demanded gruffly.

The officer repeated the story the boys had told him. The Grand Duke grew greatly interested as the story progressed, and, when the message was mentioned, he interrupted.

"Enough," he said. "I have been expecting such a message." He turned to the two lads. "Do you bear it?" he asked.

Hal bowed in assent.

"Then give it to me!" he cried eagerly.

Chester reached in his pocket, and a moment more the Grand Duke eagerly clutched the paper the lad handed him–a paper they had gone through so much to deliver.

The Grand Duke read the message through twice, sitting on his horse without a move, his face a perfect blank. Then he thrust it into his pocket and turned once more to the two lads.

"You have done well," he said. "Captain, you will see that they are brought to my quarters to-night at eight o'clock. I desire to question them. In the meantime, see that they are fed and clothed properly, for it is very cold."

The officer saluted, and the Grand Duke rode away, closely followed by the members of his staff. At a sign from the officer in whose charge they had been left, the lads followed him.

Toward the rear of the army they continued their way, coming at last upon a row of tents. Into one of these the officer led the way, the lads and the dog following him.

Here the officer quickly set out food, and the boys fell to with a will, for it was a long time since a morsel had passed their lips. Then, having satisfied their appetites, they informed the officer that they would like to rest.

The officer nodded, and showed them into another tent, where two bunks had been prepared. With a word of thanks, the boys climbed in, and the officer left them alone.

"Well," said Chester, "we have accomplished our mission successfully. What are we going to do now?"

"I have been thinking," Hal replied, "of how life on this side of the war arena would go."

"You mean stay here and not return to France?" asked Chester.

"Exactly. I have read that the Russian Cossacks are terrible fighters. I would like to see some of them in action."

"And so would I," declared Chester.

"All right," said Hal. "Then, if you are agreeable, when we see the Grand Duke to-night, I shall ask him if he cannot arrange to assign us to duties with the Russian army."

In another moment the two lads, tired out, were fast asleep, with Marquis on guard.

CHAPTER III

UNDER THE BEAR

"So, Your Excellency," Hal concluded, "you may see that we have had considerable active service."

The Russian Grand Duke Nicholas did not reply for some moments. It was plain that he was greatly impressed, as he had been greatly interested in the boys' adventures since they had taken service with the Allies just before the defense of Liège.

"Yes," he said at length, "you certainly have seen considerable service; and, in bringing me this paper safely"–the Grand Duke tapped his breast pocket–"you have rendered an invaluable service to our cause. I am indeed glad to know you. Now, if there is anything I can do to show my appreciation, you may consider it done."

Remembering their conversation of a few hours before, Hal started to speak, then hesitated. Realizing that the lad had something he felt a delicacy of saying, the Grand Duke said:

"Come, out with it. What can I do for you?"

"Well, Your Excellency," said Hal, "my friend and I would like to see service with the Russian army."

"What!" exclaimed the Grand Duke.

"Yes," Chester broke into the conversation. "We have talked it over, and we have decided that we would like to see service in the Eastern theater of war."

"Hm-m-m," said the Duke, stroking his mustache, "and have you picked out the branch of the service to which you would like to be attached?"

"Yes, sir," said Hal; "we have."

"And that is?" questioned the Grand Duke.

"The cavalry, Your Excellency–the Cossacks."

The Grand Duke jumped to his feet in surprise.

"Well, well!" he exclaimed. "You have certainly picked out the most difficult thing you could have asked me. Still, I have no doubt it can be arranged."

"If it will inconvenience you, your Excellency—" Chester began.

"Tut! Tut!" the Grand Duke interrupted him, with a wave of his hand. "It shall be done. Consider the matter settled. Do you know anything of the Cossacks?"

"Why, yes, Your Excellency," replied Hal. "We have read considerable about them."

"Still," said the Grand Duke, "I'll warrant you do not know overly much about them. I'll tell you a little, if you like."

"We would be glad to hear Your Excellency," said Chester.

"The Cossacks," said the Grand Duke, "from whom the Russian cavalry is mainly drawn, form a community within the Russian Empire enjoying special rights and privileges in return for military service. Each Cossack village holds its land as a commune, and the village assembly fixes local taxation and elects the local judges. It has been estimated that the Cossacks will place 400,000 armed men in the field in this war.

"Both in historical writings and in fiction the Cossacks are often represented as little better than savages. But this is a mistake, for the level of education among the Cossacks is higher than in the rest of Russia.

"Now, the Cossacks have always been fighters–none better in the world. They have won renown wherever they have fought by their daring and bravery. But the Cossacks, to a certain degree, are clannish–they do not take kindly to those not of their kind. Which is the reason, as I said, you had made it hard for me when you asked to be assigned to a Cossack regiment. By the way, can you ride?"

"Yes, Your Excellency," replied Hal. "We are both used to the saddle, having ridden much in America."

"Well," said the Grand Duke, "I will see that it is arranged. Report to me here in the morning."

The lads saluted and took their departure, returning to the spot where they had sought rest only a few short hours before.

15

It was about seven o'clock the following morning when they again stood in the presence of the Grand Duke. With him was an officer in a dark uniform, that gave evidence of having seen hard service, but gaily bedecked nevertheless. He was a large man, fully six feet in height, and built proportionately. The Grand Duke motioned the boys to approach.

"This," he said, indicating the officer who stood beside him, "is your future commander, General Ivan Jorvitch. I have informed him of your request, and my command that it be granted."

The lads saluted the general, and he acknowledged the salute stiffly.

"I am not at all sure as to how they will be received by the men, sir," he said to the Grand Duke.

"You will see that they are well treated," replied the Grand Duke. "My commands are not to be treated lightly. These lads will be attached to your staff with the rank of lieutenants. They are not to serve in the ranks."

"Yes, your excellency," said the general, saluting.

"You will find, general," continued the Grand Duke, "that you may depend upon them to the limit. I fancy I am a good judge of character. They have already done me an invaluable service. They may do more."

The Grand Duke then proceeded to relate some of the lads' exploits and informed the general of the message they had brought.

General Jorvitch thawed immediately upon hearing this, and extended a hand to each lad in turn.

"I shall be glad to have you with me," he told them sincerely. "I feared, at first, that the Grand Duke was trying an experiment."

In spite of the general's first gruffness the lads had taken a liking to him. Straight and erect, with a flashing eye, he was the beau ideal of a soldier. Still, there was a slight twinkle in the corner of those same eyes, which proclaimed him a man, though stern, of a kindly disposition.

The lads thanked the general, and their interview with the Grand Duke concluded, followed their new commander back to his quarters.

"I have been ordered to advance," the general informed them as they made their way along, "and as soon as I have introduced you to your fellow officers and procured you uniforms and horses, we shall proceed."

An hour later, in true Russian garb and astride two fiery chargers, the lads made their way forward with the rest of the troop. In all there were probably 10,000 Cossacks in this advance.

With one of the Cossack officers, a young lieutenant, huge in stature and pleasant of face, the lads at once struck up a friendship. He stood at least six feet six and seemed a Goliath in strength. He it was who picked their horses for them, and obtained their uniforms. Some of the other officers, while not openly hostile, still were disdainful of the two boys, and plainly not well pleased with their company.

"Have you any idea where we are bound?" asked Hal in German of their new friend, who introduced himself with a swagger as "Lieutenant Alexis Vergoff."

"Lodz; and when we get there we'll make the Germans hard to find," was the answer, made in a loud, boasting tone.

Hal and Chester glanced at each other and smiled quizzically. The same thought was in the mind of each: "He talks too boastfully to be much of a fighter."

Alexis noticed the interchange of glances, and the quizzical smiles. He realized their meaning in an instant.

"You think I won't fight, eh?" he said loudly. "Alexis Vergoff not fight? Ho! Ho!"

He threw back his head and laughed loudly. The boys were not impressed.

"Worse and more of it," thought Hal to himself.

Chester was of the same opinion, but he did not say so aloud.

"Why," continued Alexis, "I've fought more battles than you will ever hear of. I have killed twenty men."

"Twenty is a good many," said Hal softly.

"True! True!" shouted Alexis, "but I'll kill twenty more in the next battle, just to show you. You shall see what sort of a man Alexis Vergoff is!"

"I am afraid we shall see too soon," muttered Chester to himself.

"Why," went on Alexis, "it was only a month ago, before being ordered to the front, that I slew five men single-handed!"

"Great Scott!" muttered Hal. "I wish I had not started him. He'll never let up now."

"It was at my mother's home," continued Alexis. "I reached home unexpectedly. Five men had surrounded her and threatened to kill her unless she gave them money she kept in the house. One had drawn a knife just as I entered the room. No one saw me enter, and I was upon them before they knew it.

"I picked up the man with the knife as though he had been a child, and threw him bodily upon the other four. He had no time to strike at me with his knife or even drop it. The other four went down in a heap. The knife of the first man was buried in one of his companions, and so there were only three who could stagger to their feet. I picked up a lamp that stood on the table. This I hurled at another. It struck him squarely on the head, and rebounded against the head of another. Both men went down with cracked skulls. The fifth man turned to flee, but picking up a knife, I hurled it after him. It stuck in his back, and he ran half a mile before he fell down dead. The next man jumped for me—"

"Hold on!" said Hal, laughing. "You said there were only five, and you have already killed them."

"True!" muttered Alexis, though in no wise taken aback. "It was in another fight where I killed six men. I always get them mixed up. In that fight—"

"Save that for another time," said Hal, restraining his laughter with difficulty.

"Don't you want to hear it?" demanded Alexis in surprise. "I always like to hear a story of a good fight."

"I believe you would rather tell one," replied Hal.

Alexis looked very much crestfallen.

18

"Do you think I made that up?" he asked in consternation. "Why, I can tell you of other fights I have had that—"

"I don't doubt it at all," said Hal. "I am willing to admit that you can draw the long bow to the Queen's taste."

"Draw the long bow?" repeated Alexis, puzzled. "What do you mean?"

"It wouldn't do for me to tell you," replied Hal chuckling to himself. "Ask someone else."

Alexis turned to Chester.

"Do you know what he means? Will you tell me?" he asked.

"Yes, I know what he means," replied Chester, laughing, "and I believe he is right. However, it wouldn't do for me to tell you either. You must ask someone else."

Alexis turned to the man on his right, and repeated his question. The man acknowledged he knew no more what the expression meant than Alexis himself.

Alexis accosted several other officers, but with no better luck. He turned to Hal aggrieved.

"You should not have said that unless you tell me what you mean," he said.

"Ask Colonel Bluekoff, perhaps he may tell you," said Hal.

Alexis approached the Colonel.

"What is it, sir?" asked the latter.

"Colonel," said Alexis, saluting, "can you tell me what drawing the long bow means?"

The colonel looked at him in amazement. Then he said sternly:

"Get back to your place, sir. This is no time for joking."

Alexis returned to his place.

"Did he tell you?" asked Hal.

19

"No," replied Alexis, "but I'll find out, if I have to put off killing one of my enemies to ask him about it."

CHAPTER IV

LODZ

There came a sudden command from Colonel Bluekoff, and the regiment to which Hal and Chester were attached galloped forward. The advance guard could be seen falling back, firing as they retreated upon the main body of cavalry. They had encountered a force of the enemy.

With Colonel Bluekoff leading, his sword whirling about his head, the troop dashed forward at a charge. As they went by, the retreating advance guard reformed and also dashed forward with them. From ahead came several puffs of smoke and the cracking of rifles, and here and there a man fell to the ground. But the rest dashed on.

The Cossacks did not fire a shot and soon the enemy had disappeared in the distance.

"A reconnoitering force that must have gotten around Lodz in some way," Colonel Bluekoff told his officers.

The regiment now fell back upon the main body.

"That's two more," said Alexis complacently to Hal and Chester.

"Two more what?" demanded Hal.

"Two more of the enemy I have killed," said Alexis without a suspicion of a smile. "Didn't you see them go down when I fired?"

"I didn't know we fired a shot," said Chester, with a laugh.

"Sh-h-h," whispered Alexis, "do you want to get me into trouble?"

"Trouble," said Chester. "What do you mean?"

"Don't you know I'd get into trouble if the colonel knew I had fired without orders, even though I killed two of the enemy."

"Great Scott!" muttered Hal to himself. "He is the limit."

Alexis showed his revolver to Hal and Chester.

"Little invention of my own," he said. "Now I'll leave it to you, you didn't hear me when I fired, did you?"

"No," said Chester emphatically, "I did not."

"I knew it," exclaimed Alexis triumphantly. "You see," he explained, patting the revolver, "that's how I was able to kill two of the enemy without you hearing the sound of my revolver. Little invention of my own. No noise, no smoke."

Hal stretched out a hand.

"Let me have a look at that wonderful weapon," he said.

Alexis drew back, and returned the revolver quickly to its place.

"No," he said seriously. "I wouldn't trust it out of my own hand. If it's not handled just right, it might get out of commission, and I don't believe I could make another like it."

Hal whistled softly to himself.

"He's the best I ever heard," he said to himself, "and I've heard a whole lot of 'em at one time or another."

Alexis rode ahead as complacently as before, whistling softly to himself, pausing once just long enough to turn to Hal and ask:

"Have you decided yet to tell me what you mean by drawing the long bow?"

"While you have a gun like that in your possession, I wouldn't tell you for the world," replied Hal.

Now the column, at a command from General Jorvitch, increased its pace. In the distance could be made out the buildings of a large town.

"Lodz," said Alexis briefly, pointing ahead.

Hal and Chester acknowledged they understood. The troop continued onward.

Lodz, an important railroad center, was one of the most important towns in Poland, and the Grand Duke had decided that it must be held at all hazards. There was already a large body of troops stationed there, but the

Grand Duke had not considered them sufficient to hold off the ever-increasing horde of the Kaiser. Even now large masses of infantry were being thrown forward to reënforce the troops already there.

Acclaimed on all hands, the Cossacks rode rapidly through the town and went into camp at the side facing the Germans. Outposts were thrown out and the Cossacks sat down to a day of waiting.

Having secured permission, Hal, Chester and Alexis walked back toward the town. For several hours they strolled about, looking in the windows, and purchasing several small articles.

The people of Lodz were serene in their belief that there was no danger of a German invasion, in spite of the nearness of the foe. Shops and stores, theaters and all buildings were gaily decorated, and thousands promenaded the streets. The city was in festival attire.

"Looks like they were preparing for a celebration," Hal remarked to Chester.

"I should say it does," the latter returned. "But it wouldn't take the Germans long to wreck the town, if they once got here. You remember Louvain?"

"Well, they won't get here," Alexis broke in. "One Cossack is always good for ten Germans. Why, I remember—"

"Tell us later," Hal interrupted. "We want to look about a little now."

The three entered a store, where, Alexis' eye having been caught by a red necktie, the Cossack purchased it. The necktie in his pocket, he leaned over the counter and asked the salesman:

"Say, what does drawing the long bow mean?"

Hal and Chester burst into a loud guffaw, and the salesman, drawing back, suddenly turned and disappeared.

A man in civilian garb, who stood nearby, also broke into a loud guffaw. Alexis turned on him angrily.

"What are you laughing at?" he demanded.

"Why, I'm laughing at you," replied the man calmly. "What about it?"

Plainly Alexis was astonished at this reply. He drew back.

"Oh, I guess it's all right," he said pleasantly. "I wasn't sure, that's all."

"And who are these children you have with you?" demanded the man.

Hal answered this question himself.

"None of your business," he said shortly.

"Is that so?" said the man, stepping forward. "What if I should make it some of my business?"

Hal smiled.

"I don't think you will," he said quietly.

The man, large, though somewhat stout, with a red, evil-looking face, stepped quickly forward, and tapped Hal lightly on the cheek with his hand.

"Let that teach you not to talk back to your elders," he said.

"And let that teach you not to interfere in other people's business," said Hal, also taking a step forward, and tapping his opponent lightly on the cheek.

The man grew very angry, and his face turned a dull red. He raised his cane, and struck sharply at Hal. But Hal was not there, and a moment later the man received a sharp jolt on the jaw as Hal's fist went home.

The man let out a string of epithets and rushed at the boy. But the latter was prepared for him, and drove him back with straight rights and lefts; one blow brought a tiny stream of blood from the man's nose.

He drew back.

"You will answer for that," he said quietly, and turning, walked off.

Hal shrugged his shoulders, and at that moment the salesman whom Alexis had frightened a few moments before came back.

"Do you know who that was?" he asked of Hal.

"No," replied the lad, "and what's more, I don't care."

"Well," said the salesman, "the man whom you just struck is Count de Reslau, and he is very influential. You have made a bad enemy."

"I don't care if he is the King of Poland," replied Hal. "No man can hit me and get away without a return blow."

Alexis, meanwhile, had been gazing at Hal in astonishment. Now he approached and laid a hand on the lad's arm.

"A real fighter!" he exclaimed. "A man after my own heart!"

"I didn't see you doing much fighting just a moment ago," said Hal, somewhat nettled.

"Of course not," replied Alexis. "Do you think I wanted to get in trouble? Suppose an officer had come along?"

"Well," said Hal, "suppose he had?"

"If he had, we would have lost our liberty for all time to come."

"And is that why you didn't fight?"

"Yes! Discipline in the Russian army is more strict than in any army in the world; but you are certainly a fighter. The way you stood up to that man reminds me of the time I—"

"Come on," broke in Chester, not wanting to hear any more bluster, "and let's get out of here."

The three left the store, and continued their stroll about the town. As they were passing an unfrequented corner, six men suddenly sprang out upon them, armed with clubs and knives.

Hal and Chester immediately backed up against a wall, and turned to fight off their assailants; but not so Alexis.

With a loud shout he rushed upon the six who had attacked them. Right and left flew his huge fists, striking out blindly. One man toppled to the ground. A stabbing wrist was caught in the Cossack's great hand, and thrown twisting through the air. And at the same time Alexis called to Hal and Chester:

"Now you shall see how Alexis can fight!"

But Hal and Chester had no mind to let Alexis fight the whole crowd of assailants. They sprang to his aid.

Alexis drove his right fist, with tremendous power behind it, right into the face of the second man, and the latter went down to rise no more for some time to come.

Hal, with a sudden spring, clinched with one of the assailants, and the two went tumbling to the ground. Chester and another of the enemy were also rolling on the ground.

Alexis reached one huge hand and grasped another of the foe by the back of the neck, and lifted him, kicking and struggling, from his feet. The last man turned to flee, but he had reckoned without the giant Cossack.

Still holding one man by the scruff of the neck, the Cossack took a step forward and, with his free hand, grasped the last man by the back of the neck also. Then, holding one in either hand, he walked calmly to where Hal and his opponent were engaged.

Hal was uppermost, and Alexis, seizing a chance when the lad's head was out of the way, dashed the man he held in his left hand, headfirst, against the head of the enemy on the ground. There was a crunch, and both men lay still.

Then, with his other victim in his left hand, Alexis walked over to where Chester and his opponent were rolling about, and performed a similar operation. Then he lent each lad a hand in getting to his feet, after which he turned and surveyed the field of battle.

"Six!" he said briefly. "That's enough for one day. Come on! Let's get away from here before some officer comes along and sees us."

Both boys looked at the giant Cossack with amazement written large upon their faces. From the first time that he had boasted to them, they had put him down as anything but a fighter, in spite of his huge size. But the quickness with which he had disposed of six men showed them that they had been wrong.

As they walked along, it was plain to the lads that something was troubling Alexis; and at last Hal was moved to ask:

"What's the matter, Alexis?"

The huge Cossack looked at the lad for a moment, and then said:

"There is no use my telling you, but I will. I want to know what you meant by 'drawing the long bow.'"

CHAPTER V

ALEXIS IN BATTLE

Both lads laughed heartily.

"You'll learn before many days," said Hal, "and I am not as sure as I was about it."

"Nor I," agreed Chester.

The three made their way back to their posts, where Alexis immediately insisted on donning his new red necktie. Marquis, who had been left behind while the three friends made a tour of the city, greeted them with joyful barks. He had made friends with the big Cossack, and the latter had taken quite a fancy to the dog.

Hardly had the three retired to their positions, when an air of excitement throughout the troops became apparent. There was bustle and some slight confusion and shouted commands. A moment later and a body of 5,000 Cossacks, armed and spurred, stood beside their horses, ready to mount and ride at the command.

"Where do you suppose we are going?" asked Hal of Chester.

"Haven't any idea," was the reply, "but it looks as though there was a little fighting to be done."

"That's what!" exclaimed Alexis, who stood beside the two lads. "Now you shall see how we handle the Germans."

"Mount!" came the command.

As one man, the troop sprang to the saddle.

"Forward!" came the next order, and the Cossacks started forward at a gallop.

Good riders themselves, Hal and Chester could not but envy the riding prowess of their companions. Accounted among the best riders in the world, the Cossacks who now dashed forward hurled themselves toward the enemy with reckless abandon. Their lances held high in one hand, each brandished a large revolver in his other. The bridles lay across the horses' necks, the riders guiding their mounts by the pressure of their knees.

And so they swept forward, dashing swiftly over the few miles of open ground toward the spot where the Germans were known to be entrenched.

The enemy greeted them with a hail of bullets, but they faltered not. Men fell and horses dropped, but there was no hesitation among those left.

Now a bugle sounded, and they dashed on with greater ferocity than before.

Squadrons of German cavalry issued forth to meet them. They crashed with a terrible shock. The impact was terrific, and horses and riders on both sides reeled back.

But the Cossacks were the first to recover, and they spurred their horses into the thick of the enemy. The sweep of their lances and the fire from their automatics were deadly. There was no pause in the Russian attack.

Cutting and slashing, the squadron to which Hal, Chester and Alexis were attached was soon in the midst of the foe. Not unused to such encounters, the lads nevertheless found themselves hard put to keep their seats and ward off the blows of their foes.

But with each moment they gained confidence, and finally were fighting with the best of them. Hal caught a descending lance on his upraised sword, and raising his revolver took a snap shot at his opponent. The latter threw his arms high, and toppled from his horse. Chester, by a quick move, escaped a revolver shot aimed at him by a German officer, and the lad's own weapon spoke sharply. His aim was true, and the German dropped.

Now the Germans began to give ground. It was impossible to stand in the face of the terrible Cossack charge. The Russians pressed the retreating foe closely.

But now new forces of Germans dashed forward to drive back the Cossacks, or at least to protect the retreat of their companions.

The Cossacks dashed into these fresh troops with the same abandon they had first charged. But this time the result was different. Tired by the furious work, they were thrown back by the German reënforcements, and in spite of heroic efforts, were forced to retire slowly.

Flushed with this success, the Germans pressed on. The fighting was man to man, horse to horse, and hand to hand. Not for once had Alexis left the side of the two lads and none of the three had so far been injured, although men dropped on all sides of them.

Suddenly there came a command from Colonel Bluekoff.

"Charge!" he cried.

Immediately the squadron to which the lads were attached hurled itself forward once more, right into the thickest of the fray, in the face of overwhelming numbers. They dashed forward with the fury of madmen, shouting and yelling as they charged.

For a moment the Germans gave back, so terrible was the charge of this mere handful of Cossacks, but for a moment only; then they came on again. From all sides they bore down on the squadron, now completely cut off from the main body of troops, seeking to annihilate them.

There was no order to surrender from the German commander, nor would one have been heeded for the matter of that. At a quick command, the Cossacks formed a little square, back to back, and awaited the attack of the enemy.

It came upon the instant. Upon the Russian horsemen the Germans hurled themselves bravely, cutting and shooting as they came on. The Cossacks gave blow for blow, and in spite of the fierce charge, maintained their unbroken front, though men fell here and there. Unable to pierce this line of steel, the Germans drew off.

Given this little breathing space, Hal and Chester, standing side by side, took in the scene about them. Of the little troop of Cossacks there remained now possibly a hundred men. Their support, the lads could see, desperately engaged elsewhere, would be unable to come to their assistance. It was up to them to fight it out alone.

Colonel Bluekoff was down, having been pierced a few moments before by a German bullet. Among these few men there were, besides Alexis, but two minor officers unharmed. At that moment Alexis himself took command.

His sword raised aloft, he turned flashing eyes upon his men.

"Will we surrender?" he shouted, and answered his own question: "No!"

A wild cheer from his men was the reply. The huge Cossack turned to the two lads.

"We will fight till the last," he said calmly. "Are you with us?"

"We are," said Hal simply.

"You bet!" Chester agreed.

"Good!" exclaimed Alexis.

He turned once more toward the enemy, who, it was evident, were preparing for another attack upon the little band. The latter stood quietly, awaiting the charge; and in a moment it came.

Urging their horses on at a gallop, the Germans came rapidly forward. There was the clash of steel on steel as the enemy hurled themselves upon three sides of the little square simultaneously. Russians and Germans dropped together, fighting till the last.

But the odds against them were too great. Dense masses of the Germans swooped down upon them, engulfing them, overpowering them. Hal, engaged with a big German officer, had just succeeded in parrying a thrust of the other's sword, when someone from behind struck him a heavy blow over the head. The lad fell from his horse without a sound.

Chester, seeing his friend fall, fought his way toward Hal. He was just about to leap from his horse by his chum's side, when a tall German trooper brought the flat of his sword down on the lad's head. Chester also went hurtling to the ground.

And now Alexis, with a few remaining men, was left to fight the enemy alone. His sword whirling around his head in great sweeps, and an empty revolver clutched tightly in his left hand; his teeth bared in a snarl and his eyes flashing angrily, this great Cossack stood off his foes.

Four men sprang upon him at once. Putting spurs to his horse, the giant dashed in between them. Two he cut down with lightning-like slashes of his sword, and a third he disposed of by hurling his empty revolver squarely into his face. The sword of the fourth pierced him through the left arm, but before the German could regain his balance after this thrust, Alexis' sweeping sword had laid him low also.

The giant Cossack was now the last of his troop in condition to fight. Suddenly his horse staggered, and went to its knees. With a quick move, Alexis freed himself and leaped from the saddle just as the animal, dying from a pistol wound in its head, toppled to the ground.

Alexis leaped up lightly and turned again to face his foes.

31

A German officer urged his horse forward, seeking to ride him down. As the horse approached, Alexis fell on one knee, and the horse, pierced by his sword, fell to the ground. The officer leaped from the animal's back, but before he could bring his revolver to bear upon Alexis, the latter had pierced him through with a thrust of his sword.

A dozen of the enemy sprang upon him. With his sword sweeping around his head, seeming to make a circle of fire, the great Cossack held them at bay. One ventured to spring at him, and without even stopping the whirl of his weapon, Alexis dropped him at his feet.

More Germans sprang to the attack–ten, twenty, thirty of them. Hopelessly outnumbered, and believing that the end was near, Alexis gave up his defensive tactics and leaped into the very midst of his foes. For a moment they gave way before him, then closed in again like a pack of hungry wolves. Here and there the giant's sword darted out and men dropped beneath its thrust.

Cutting and thrusting with his dripping sword, and striking out with his naked fist, Alexis fought on. A sword pierced him through the shoulder, but the man who had aimed the thrust paid the penalty with his life. Two men closed in, and as the Cossack struck out at the one on his left with his fist, the second German seized his sword arm.

With a roar like that of an angry bull, Alexis gave a mighty wrench, and the sword came free. At the same moment he felt a sting in his right arm. A bullet had struck him. The giant scarcely felt his wounds, although he was bleeding now in a dozen places. Before him, the ground was full of dark swaying faces. His sword found another human sheath, and being unable to withdraw it quickly enough to meet another of his foes, he left it there and turned upon his enemies with his bare hands.

He snatched a revolver from the ground, and not taking time to aim, dashed it into the face of the nearest man, and then dashed forward, hitting out with his naked fists.

Vaguely he noticed the sameness of the faces about him. A short wiry man sprang at him, and with a broken sword, stabbed him in the left shoulder. Alexis caught him by the throat with his right hand, and the man gave a choking screech as he lifted him clear off the ground.

As he did so, someone behind him struck him a heavy blow on the head with the butt of a revolver. With a last furious effort he turned upon his foes, and dashed the man he held by the throat full into their faces; fell forward upon the body and, with a great sob, he shuddered and lay still.

And there, on the battlefield on the plains of Poland, lay the bodies of the two American lads and, a short distance away, that of Alexis, the giant Cossack, their friend.

CHAPTER VI

MARQUIS

The Russian cavalry, outnumbered by the Germans, had continued to give ground and the Germans were still in pursuit. But now, from the distance arose a cloud of dust, and a moment later, in a headlong dash to save their companions, came a second body of Cossack cavalry, 5,000 strong, to give battle to the Germans.

Down they came upon the unprepared Germans, with yells and shouts, their horses running free. At the same time that part of the first Cossack body which still remained reformed and sprang forward.

The Germans turned and fled.

Then from the trenches came forth columns of infantry, supported by field batteries, and in a moment these had opened upon the advancing Russian horsemen; but in spite of this hail of death, the Cossacks did not falter nor pause. Straight up to the mouth of the field guns they rode–sabering the gunners right and left–and in a few moments these had been silenced.

Then the Cossacks turned their attention to the infantry, which, firing with machine-like precision and accuracy, dealt havoc to the ranks of the Russian horsemen and mowed them down.

Several squadrons of Cossacks dismounted and approached the foe on foot, and soon the fighting became hand to hand. The standard-bearer suddenly threw up his hands and fell over backward, the colors fluttering to the ground.

A German officer, thinking to capture the flag, jumped forward, and leaning down laid his hand upon it; but at that moment a hairy, snarling body sprang forward, straight at the German's throat. The latter released his hold on the flag and jumped to his feet to ward off the attack of this strange enemy, which he could not at first make out.

But this new enemy was not to be shaken off. His teeth found their mark, and with a cry, the German tumbled to earth.

The newcomer was Marquis.

Separated from Hal and Chester, Marquis, though a battle dog, had become uneasy at their absence and set out to find them. He had advanced with the

34

second troop of Cossacks, and seeing the dead upon the field, had been trying to pick out the bodies of the two lads.

But when the Russian standard-bearer, almost beside him, had been shot down and the German had leaped for the colors, Marquis had turned from the search of his friends to dispose of his lifelong enemy.

As Marquis' foe went to the ground, a second German sprang forward and, aiming a kick at the dog, also stooped and started to raise the colors. Marquis, disregarding the kick, seized upon the flag with his teeth at the same moment.

Then came a tug of war. Snarling, and with bristling back, Marquis pulled at the standard. Crying out hoarse epithets, the German pulled also; but neither made any headway.

Realizing that the dog was a match for him, the German uttered a fierce imprecation, dropped his hold on the flag, stepped back and aimed his revolver.

But the dog was ready for him. He had released his hold upon the flag almost as soon as had the German, and his canine reasoning told him the German's object. Before the German could pull the trigger, Marquis was ready for him, and hurled his body straight at the German's throat.

He had gauged the distance accurately enough, and beneath the shock the officer was hurled to the ground. He attempted to fight off his four-footed assailant, but he was no match for the angry dog.

This adversary disposed of, Marquis calmly returned to the flag, picked it up in his mouth, carried it to the commander of the squadron and put it in his hand. The commander took the time to pat Marquis on the head, and utter some words of praise.

But Marquis had no time to listen to these. He had other work to do, and had disappeared almost before the Cossack ceased speaking.

Hither and thither over the field of battle Marquis made his way, sniffing the bodies of the dead, and licking the faces of the wounded. For an hour he wandered about, and at last his search was rewarded.

From near him came a feeble moan. Marquis pricked up his ears. Surely he recognized that voice. The moan came again. Marquis hesitated no longer.

He had recognized the voice of Hal. Quickly he sprang to where the lad lay and poked his cold muzzle into the boy's face.

Hal turned feebly on his side and put out a hand before he realized what had touched him. Then he succeeded in raising himself on one arm and threw the other around Marquis' neck.

"Marquis!" he almost sobbed. "Where is Chester?"

Apparently the dog understood his question, for he jumped away and began nosing other bodies nearby. And at last he came upon Chester. The latter also was returning to consciousness. With some difficulty Hal staggered to his feet and made his way to his friend's side. He turned to Marquis.

"Get some water!" he commanded, and paused to see if the dog understood.

Marquis bounded away, and returned a few moments later with a well-filled canteen, in his mouth. Hastily Hal removed the stopper and poured some of the water down Chester's throat. Then he took a drink himself.

Thus refreshed, Chester sat up and looked around. Hal did the same. It was indeed a terrible sight that met their eyes. As far as they could see, bodies of dead and wounded men lay scattered about. Hal shuddered.

"Terrible!" he exclaimed. Then: "I wonder where Alexis is?" He turned to Marquis. "Find Alexis," he commanded.

Marquis understood and trotted away. Chester and Hal now arose and walked slowly after him. At last Marquis, some distance away, set up a loud bark. Hal and Chester approached as rapidly as their exhausted condition would permit.

Marquis was standing directly over the body of the giant Cossack, surrounded by a circle of the enemies whom Alexis had slain in combat.

The giant stirred slightly as the boys approached. Quickly Hal bent over him and, raising his head upon his knee, placed the canteen to his lips.

This brought a sigh from Alexis' lips, and soon he sat up and looked around.

"Well," said he, waving his arm toward the circle of his fallen foes, "you can see what a Cossack does when he fights."

"I see," said Hal briefly. "But come, if you are able to walk. We had better get away from this spot. The battle is not over."

Alexis objected.

"What, a Cossack run!" he demanded.

"But if we stay here we shall probably be killed," replied Chester. "See," pointing, "even now the Cossacks are retreating in the face of superior numbers. We must go."

"I don't—" began Alexis, but Hal interrupted him.

"Come on," he said, taking him by the arm. "Let's move away from here."

Grumbling and protesting, the giant allowed himself to be led toward the head of the Cossack line, now some distance back. Bullets and shells were still whistling overhead, for the three were between the opposing forces. None dropped near them, however, and they continued on their way.

Suddenly, from the German line, came the clear call of a bugle.

"Quick!" shouted Hal, hurrying forward. "The Germans are going to charge. We mustn't be caught in between."

But it was too late. Even as the lad spoke, the German cavalry came forward with a rush.

Hal realized in an instant that they would not have time to rejoin the main body of Cossacks, for should the latter advance to meet the charge, they would not do so rapidly enough to come up to them before the Germans. Should the Cossacks retreat, the three could not possibly hope to come up with them.

Fortunately the three were at the extreme east of the battle line; so now, turning quickly, Hal led the way out of danger. When far enough away so that there was little likelihood of being struck by stray bullets, they halted to witness the progress of the battle.

The Cossacks advanced to meet the charge of the German cavalry, and threw it back upon its infantry support, which once more issued from the trenches. German field guns were unlimbered and hurled their shells screeching at the Russians. The latter were forced to retreat.

The Germans pushed this advantage closely.

"If we only had infantry or artillery here," groaned Alexis, "there would be a different story to tell."

"I'm sure of that," replied Hal; "but to advance in the face of such overwhelming numbers would be foolish."

"True," said Alexis, "but I never like to see a Cossack run from his foes, no matter what their number."

It was plain now that the Russian commander realized the futility of further fighting with his vastly superior foe. The Cossacks gave way more rapidly and finally turned and began their retreat upon Lodz.

"And here we are right in the middle of the Germans," said Chester. "What are we going to do?"

"We'll have to try to get back to our lines," said Hal, "and the sooner we start the better."

"Good," said Chester. "Let's start at once."

Alexis had so far recovered now as to announce that he was feeling "perfectly fit," and making a slight detour, the three friends, closely followed by Marquis, set out.

They had progressed possibly half a mile, when Marquis suddenly began to growl.

"What do you suppose is the matter with him?" demanded Chester.

"I don't know," replied Hal. "Evidently he scents some kind of danger." He turned to the dog. "What is it, Marquis?" he demanded.

Marquis' only answer was a series of deep growls.

"Germans?" asked Hal.

Marquis uttered a short bark.

"That's what's the matter," said Hal, quietly.

At that moment there came riding down a nearby road a troop of German cavalry.

"Quick! down on the ground!" cried Hal. "Perhaps they won't see us!"

He suited the action to the word, and Chester and Alexis followed his example.

But it was too late. The Germans had espied them and now came toward them at a gallop. Alexis rose to his feet and stretched.

"Another fight," he said. "Good!"

"Fight nothing!" exclaimed Hal. "It's impossible. They have us. That's all there is about it. We shall have to submit."

The Germans came to a sudden halt a few feet away, and rifles were brought to bear upon the three friends.

"You are our prisoners!" called the German commander.

CHAPTER VII

GERMANY'S NAPOLEON

Hal raised his hands in token of surrender.

"There is no help for it," he said to his two friends in an undertone.

The German commander motioned the three to approach. They did so.

"You will each climb up behind one of my men," ordered the German leader.

Hal and Chester did as ordered, but when Alexis approached one of the German horsemen the latter eyed him dubiously.

"Man!" he exclaimed. "You can't ride with me. You would break this horse in two."

The officer turned to the soldier.

"Give your horse to the prisoner," he commanded, "and you climb up behind the man nearest you."

The soldier did as commanded, and a moment later Alexis also was in the saddle. Then the little troop got under way again, headed for the German lines.

There was no conversation as the little troop rode along, and at length they were well inside the German trenches. Here, after some delay, the three prisoners were conducted before General von Hindenburg, the Teuton commander in the East, a man of kindly face and courteous bearing, the man whose successes, brief though they were, earned him the name of "The German Napoleon."

"How comes it," asked General von Hindenburg of Hal, "that you two American lads are fighting with the Russians? How comes it that two lads born and reared in a civilized country have espoused the cause of the barbarians?"

"In the first place," answered Hal boldly, "I do not consider the Russians barbarians. In the next place, we joined the Allies when the Germans ravaged Belgium."

"Ravaged!" exclaimed the German commander with some heat.

"Exactly," said Hal. "We joined the Belgian army before Liège, and we hold commissions in the Belgian army. We were also attached for a time to the British forces under Sir John French. We bore communications from Sir John French to Grand Duke Nicholas, that is how we happen to be here."

"And how did you carry these dispatches, may I ask?" inquired General von Hindenburg.

"By airship," replied Hal briefly.

"What!" cried the general. "You flew over Germany in an airship?"

"Well, only part of it," replied Hal with a grin; and seeing no harm, he told the German commander of their adventures after being captured and taken to Berlin.

"You are brave lads," said the general calmly, when Hal had finished. "I would that Germany had more like you. But I fear your fighting days are over."

"What will you do with us, General?" asked Chester, who up to this time had remained silent, Hal usually acting as spokesman when there was explaining to be done.

"You will be sent to Posen," replied the general, "where you will be detained until after the war."

"But that may be for years, General," protested Hal, trying to draw the general out.

In this he was successful.

"You are mistaken," replied General von Hindenburg calmly. "The war will be over within the next six months. Germany will have conquered."

Hal did not reply, for he had no mind to antagonize the general; but he had his own ideas as to the ultimate outcome of the war.

The general now summoned one of his staff, and turned the lads over to the latter with this injunction:

"Have them sent to Posen. Instruct Commander Friech that they must be well guarded, but treated with kindness."

He bowed gravely to both lads, who saluted and followed the other officer from the German commander's quarters.

"You will remain in my quarters until to-night," said the officer to the three friends, "and you probably will start on your journey about midnight. There is a detachment leaving about that time."

He conducted the three and the dog to his tent, where their wounds were dressed and a guard was stationed over them. Then they were left to themselves.

Alexis, who up to this time had not spoken, at last opened his mouth.

"What's this all about?" he demanded. "I can't understand this outlandish gibberish. What's it all about, anyhow?"

The conversation between the lads and the German officers had been in English.

Chester broke into a laugh.

"Outlandish gibberish!" he exclaimed. "Why, Alexis, if you only knew how your native tongue sounds, you wouldn't call anything gibberish. It's fortunate you speak German."

"Well, perhaps so," Alexis agreed. "But what's it all about?"

"Simply," said Hal, "that we are to be taken to Posen, where we will be held prisoners till after the war."

Alexis uttered a loud Russian imprecation.

"I was in hope," he said, "that when I went into East Prussia it would be as part of an army too big for the Germans ever to drive out."

"It can't be helped now," said Chester briefly.

"It would have been helped if you had let me fight when I wanted to," said the big Cossack regretfully.

All day long the three were kept close inside the tent. Not once were they permitted to step into the open. Night fell, and food was placed before them. They were almost famished, so they ate heartily, sharing their meal with

Marquis. It was well along toward midnight when the German officer once more entered the tent and informed them it was time for them to leave.

They followed the officer into the open air, where a large body of men were ready to move. Quickly they were led to horses, and were soon in the saddle. Then, closely guarded, they were led away at a swift trot.

The German camp was some miles from the nearest railroad station, and it took several hours to cover this distance. At last, however, they were conducted aboard a train, where, under heavy guard, they continued their journey.

It was well along toward the next evening when the train, after many stops, finally pulled into Posen. With a number of other prisoners, the three friends and Marquis, who had been allowed to accompany them, were taken from the train and turned over to another squad of troops. In the center of these they were led to a large and massive castle at one end of the town. Here they were thrust into a dark though well-appointed room, which, their guard informed them, was to be their prison.

"So this is where we are to spend the next few years, eh?" said Chester.

"The outlook is not very bright," replied Hal, "but we shall have to make the best of a bad situation."

The three began a careful survey of their prison. There were two large windows in the room, looking out into a little court. Through these a dim light streamed. The windows were heavily barred. Hal and Chester tested the bars. Alexis, however, after one look, sat down in deep disgust. If his wounds bothered him any, he did not seem to mind them.

"No chance of escape here," said Hal, after shaking one of the heavy iron bars.

"I should say not," agreed Chester, after making a test.

They turned from the windows just as a key grated in the lock of the heavy door, and a man of huge stature, topping the giant frame of Alexis by more than an inch, entered the room.

"Good evening," he said politely enough. "I have come to see if you require anything. We have been instructed to treat you kindly."

"A little liberty is about all," said Hal, with a rueful smile.

"I am sorry," replied the newcomer, also smiling slightly, "but that is the one thing I cannot grant you. I suppose you wonder who I am?"

The boys nodded.

"I," said the newcomer, striking himself a hard blow on the chest, "am Freiderich von Bernstrum, brother of Heinrich von Bernstrum, commander of this fortress, and I am kept cooped up here while there is fighting to be done–me, Freiderich von Bernstrum, a real fighter!"

"Hm-m-m," muttered Hal to himself as he glanced keenly at Alexis. "Two of a kind."

Alexis moved restlessly as the big German made this boast. It was plain to both lads that, while he might like to brag himself, he did not relish hearing another do so.

"Yes," continued von Bernstrum, "I would go to the front. But my brother, he would stay here. You see," and the talkative German leaned closer to the lads, "he has a fair captive in the tower above, and he seeks to marry her."

"And who is she?" demanded Hal.

"I will mention no names," replied the German. "Enough that she is a Russian countess."

Alexis jumped to his feet and advanced upon the big German.

"You have dared to lay a hand upon a Russian lady?" he demanded.

The German eyed him amusedly.

"And what of it?" he demanded. "However, you need have no fear. She prefers me, and I shall take her away from him."

Alexis raised a threatening hand, but Hal stayed him.

"Quiet," he whispered. "Some good may come of this if you obey me."

Alexis subsided.

Hal approached Chester and whispered.

"Keep von Bernstrum in conversation while I have a word with Alexis."

44

Chester did as Hal ordered, and the latter whispered to the big Cossack:

"Do you think you can whip this man?" pointing to von Bernstrum.

Alexis' fingers twitched.

"Remember you are wounded, Alexis."

"Try me," he said simply.

"Keep quiet, then, and do as I tell you," said Hal.

He turned again to von Bernstrum.

"I can see," he said, "that the lady would be pleased to know a man like you."

"Ah! you see it?" cried the German. "But Heinrich is so cunning. Now if I had your help—"

"What would you have us do?" asked Hal.

The big German was silent for some minutes before replying.

"If I had your help," he said at length, "I would see that you all regained your liberty. Will you help me?"

"What is it you would have us do?" asked Chester.

"I will not say until you have promised," said von Bernstrum.

"And we will not promise till you have told us," said Hal. "How do we know that you are a man of your word, or that you are a fighter, such as you would have us believe."

"What! Freiderich von Bernstrum not a fighter!" exclaimed the big German in surprise.

"We have only your word for it," said Hal quietly.

Von Bernstrum paced up and down excitedly. He stopped suddenly.

"Let me bring swords!" he exclaimed, "and you shall see whether I can fight!"

He made as if to leave the room.

45

"Not so fast!" exclaimed Hal. "The clash of steel would bring the whole fortress down on us. But I shall try you out."

"How?" exclaimed the German eagerly.

"Alexis!" called Hal.

The big Cossack approached.

"Here," said Hal to the German, pointing to Alexis, "is a foeman worthy of your steel. You shall try with him."

"Good!" exclaimed von Bernstrum. "With fists?"

"No," replied Hal, who was somewhat doubtful of Alexis' prowess in the fistic art. "How about a wrestling match?"

"Good!" exclaimed von Bernstrum again. "But I assure you I am his superior." He turned to Alexis. "Get ready, man!"

CHAPTER VIII

THE ESCAPE

Alexis made ready.

Hal realized that he was taking a desperate chance to put through the scheme that had entered his mind. Not only was von Bernstrum a bigger man than Alexis, but the latter had lost much blood only 36 hours before. Doubtless also he knew every trick of a wrestler or fighter.

Alexis took off his shoes and threw them into a corner, and divested himself of his coat. Von Bernstrum growled like a dog as he followed the Cossack's example.

Alexis held out his hand. Von Bernstrum gripped it hard and gave a grunt of satisfaction.

"A man's hand," he exclaimed.

Alexis placed his right hand across the German's shoulders and caught him firmly and the boys saw by the expression on his face that he was not certain of the outcome. The German had not boasted in vain. He was indeed a giant.

"If ever men felt the joy of battle, these two do," exclaimed Hal to Chester.

The two men were now gripped in a tight embrace. Von Bernstrum felt Alexis over carefully, but gave him no opening.

"A man's chest," he grunted.

Alexis so far had uttered no word. Now he perceived that his opponent was preparing for the loin throw and prepared himself to meet it. When he had foiled this attack, he held his opponent for a moment at a disadvantage.

Alexis gripped von Bernstrum for a hug. Had the German been a weaker man, his ribs must have cracked; but he had caught deep breath, and the Cossack might as well have tried to crush a tree.

"A good try!" muttered the German.

He now tested Alexis sorely. He tried a cross hitch, but failed. At this, a smile broke out on Alexis' face.

47

Both lads, who had been watching the struggle nervously, now grew confident. It was evident that the Cossack hoped for victory.

At last Alexis saw his chance. In getting the grip he wanted, it was necessary for him to face the danger of putting himself in his opponent's power; but the Cossack ventured to do this, for he realized that by no other means could he throw him. Von Bernstrum saw his opponent's move and took advantage of it, and for a moment Alexis was afraid it was all over with him.

But he still held his ground. Von Bernstrum's grip grew weaker at last, and the boys could hear him panting like a dog. Hal spoke to Chester.

"I believe he realizes that Alexis will master him," he exclaimed in a whisper.

Chester nodded in assent.

Now Alexis put all the strength of his mighty shoulders, back and loins into a mighty heave, and Freiderich von Bernstrum, giant though he was, went flying across the room, his head striking the floor with a terrible thud.

For a moment the lads were afraid Alexis had killed him; but for a moment only. Calmly Alexis put on his shoes and donned his coat. Then he turned to his young friends and waited. His attitude said as plain as words:

"I have done the fighting. You do the rest."

Quickly Hal stooped over the fallen man and took a bunch of keys from his pocket. Then, straightening up, he approached the door, opened it and peered out. There was no one in sight.

Hal turned to Alexis.

"Change clothes with him," he whispered, motioning to the fallen German.

Hastily Alexis obeyed. In spite of the fact that von Bernstrum was almost two inches taller than Alexis, the height of the latter was so great that Hal believed the difference would not be noticed.

The lad now relieved von Bernstrum of his revolvers. Alexis had donned his adversary's sword with his uniform. Then once more Hal approached the door and peered out. Then he spoke to Alexis.

"We will go with you as though we were your prisoners," he explained. "If anyone accosts us, we may have to fight. However, I believe you look enough like von Bernstrum to avoid detection. Pull the hat well over your face, and if anyone asks where you are going, reply that you are taking the prisoners to the commandant. Do you understand?"

Alexis signified that he did, and quietly the three, still followed by Marquis, left the room. Along the same passageways they had traversed Hal guided Alexis by a touch of the hand, for the lad's sense of direction was much better than that of the giant Cossack.

At last they came into the open and started toward the gate. So far they had not been accosted. At the gate a soldier approached Alexis and saluted.

"Are you going out, sir?" he demanded.

"Yes," replied the Cossack, mimicking von Bernstrum's voice as best he could. "These prisoners have given me their parole, and I am taking them out for a breath of air. Get me two more horses."

The soldier saluted and turned away. Hal addressed Alexis.

"You are doing beautifully," he exclaimed. "I didn't know you were such a strategist."

"Why," exclaimed Alexis, "next to being a fighter I am a strategist. I remember one time—"

"Save it for some other time," said Hal.

"If you don't believe—" began the big Cossack, somewhat crestfallen.

"Never mind now," broke in Chester. "We have other things to do."

Alexis subsided, grumbling. A few moments later the soldier reappeared leading three horses. Alexis took all three bridles, and bade the soldier begone, which order the latter obeyed in a hurry.

Quickly the three friends leaped into the saddle, and started off at a rapid trot, riding eastward. Out of sight of the town, they bore off slightly to the North, for, as Hal said, they did not wish to run right into the German army advancing on Lodz.

They had proceeded perhaps a mile out of sight of the castle, when Hal suddenly checked his mount, and raised a warning hand. All stopped to listen. From the direction in which they had just come, came the frenzied tolling of a great bell, followed by a few faint shots.

"They have learned of our escape," said Hal quietly. "That, I imagine, is a warning to the countryside to be on the lookout for us."

All three put spurs to their horses, and set off again at a gallop. For two hours they kept up this swift pace, and then Alexis drew rein.

"Unless I want this horse to drop under me," he said, "we shall have to slow down. There is no horse living that can carry me at that gait very long."

The boys did not doubt this, and they continued their journey at a more leisurely pace. Finally, rounding a turn in the road, they came upon a little stream, perhaps a hundred yards wide. There was no bridge.

"Guess we shall have to make our horses swim it," said Chester.

Accordingly all plunged into the stream, Marquis swimming behind, and soon reached the opposite shore. Here they drew up in a clump of bushes and sat down to dry off a bit.

"Do you suppose they know which way we came?" asked Hal of Chester.

"I don't know. However, I suppose they will search in all directions, and they are bound to come upon us sooner or later if we linger around here."

"You are right. I guess we had better move."

Soon the little party was in the saddle again, and making off at a rapid trot. Hal, for some unaccountable reason turning suddenly in his saddle, uttered an ejaculation.

"What's the matter?" demanded Chester.

"Look!" said Hal, pointing back toward the little stream.

Alexis and Chester followed the direction of Hal's finger. Just plunging into the stream were half a dozen horsemen, and it was plain from that distance that they were German soldiers, and that they had made out the forms of the fugitives.

The three friends put spurs to their horses and, with Marquis loping along behind, soon lost themselves in a little woods. Here they urged their tired

50

horses on, and at last came to a small open space. This they crossed before Alexis' horse gave out and went to the ground in a heap.

"I am afraid it's all off," exclaimed Hal. "How far do you suppose we are from the German border, Alexis?"

"Not far," answered the Cossack. "Besides, some of our troops have been operating in these parts. They were only small detachments, and most of them have been driven off; but even now there may be some of them near."

Alexis urged the two lads to ride on and leave him, but this they refused to do. Therefore they dismounted and, turning their horses loose, they continued their journey on foot.

As they walked along a man suddenly popped out from among the trees, brought his revolver to bear upon the trio, and in a loud tone cried:

"Halt!"

Alexis gave one quick glance at the man's uniform, uttered a cry of pleasure and spoke a few quick words in his native tongue. The lads were surprised to see the man drop his rifle, throw his arms about Alexis and embrace him.

For some moments after quitting this embrace the two talked in Russian, the lads being able to pick up only a few words. Then Alexis turned to the two lads.

"My brother," he said simply. "He belongs to a detachment of Cossacks who raided in these parts two weeks ago. The detachment was surrounded by Germans, he tells me, and practically annihilated. About 150 men escaped to the woods, where they have been conducting a guerilla warfare, picking off the Germans one at a time, wherever they happen to find one alone, or in pairs, or small parties. These Cossacks are scattered all through the woods, and to get them together would be almost impossible."

"Then how are they able to tell friend from foe?"

"You see that large green leaf my brother wears in his hat?"

"Yes."

"That is their emblem."

Alexis' brother approached and spoke in German.

"Come," he said. "I shall show you something."

He led the way into the woods, and approached a large tree, where he pointed to a placard tacked on it. The placard read:

"All Russians at large in these woods are ordered to assemble at this spot the 10th of this month without arms and surrender, under penalty of death."

"That was posted two weeks ago," said Alexis' brother, "and this is the 20th. Read our answer below it."

The answer read:

"Come and take us!"

CHAPTER IX

GUERILLA WARFARE

"Do you mean?" asked Hal, "that 150 men, at large in these woods, have defied the whole German army?"

"There are less than a hundred now," replied the brother of Alexis, whose name the lads learned was Stephan. "We have been conducting this guerilla warfare for more than two weeks now, and we have done inestimable harm to the Germans. We have evaded large bodies of troops sent out to kill or capture us. Of course, some of our men have been picked off, but we are not going to run yet."

"But how do you live?" demanded Chester.

"We have been living on roots and herbs," was the reply, "and such other food as we have been able to take from the enemy."

"And where do you sleep?"

"This forest," said Stephan, "makes an ideal hiding place. It is filled with large caves, the presence of which seems to be unknown to the foe. Many of the caves are large enough for twenty men, although it is seldom that there are more than five or six men in one at a time."

From the rear came the sound of galloping horses. Stephan sprang to instant action.

"Come with me," he cried, and led the way into the very thick of the forest.

Hal, Chester, Alexis and Marquis followed him and soon were safe from discovery in a large cave, the mouth of which was screened from view by a dense mass of shrubbery.

Outside, after a few minutes, the lads could hear the sounds of moving horses and the exclamations of their riders. The horsemen halted near the entrance to the cave and held a consultation.

"They have probably fallen in with some of these guerillas," said one voice. "If so, we shall have hard work to find them."

Close upon his words came a scream from outside, and straining their ears, the party inside made out the sound of a distant pistol shot.

"One more gone," said Stephan briefly.

There came a volley from outside the cave, as the Germans fired at their unseen assailant.

"Not much chance of their hitting anybody," said Stephan calmly.

From outside the cave came the sound of rapidly retreating hoofbeats. The Germans were moving away. Alexis, having thus quickly learned the way of the guerillas, cautiously poked his head from the cave, reached back and picked up his brother's rifle, and fired after the retreating foe.

"Another one," he said grimly, returning the weapon to Stephan.

"Just how long do you suppose you can keep this work up?" Chester asked of Stephan.

"Not much longer, I am afraid," was the reply. "I figure it is only a question of days now until the Germans send out a force strong enough to search the woods thoroughly. In that event, we shall try to make our way back over the border to safety."

From a corner of the cave Stephan now produced a small quantity of food, which he set out. All fell to and it was soon disposed of. Then they ventured from the cave and, walking slowly, made their way northward.

"It's just a case of keep moving," Stephan explained. "Of course, it might be possible for us to join forces, but then we should greatly lessen our effectiveness."

Alexis, who was in front, stopped suddenly and threw up a warning hand. Immediately the other three halted in their tracks. Peering in the direction in which Alexis pointed, they made out the forms of half a dozen German soldiers standing near a tree. Directly, however, the latter made off, and the little party approached the tree.

"Another placard, eh?" muttered Stephan, as he drew near.

The other three also approached and read:

"The time for surrender has been extended till to-morrow at noon!"

Angrily, Stephan snatched the placard from the tree. Turning, he saw several other trees also bearing placards. These he also tore down.

"Surrender, eh!" he cried. "Never!"

Suddenly he clapped his hand to his side and staggered back. At the same instant, from directly ahead, came the sharp crack of a rifle. But Stephan did not fall. Recovering himself, he dashed straight in the direction of the shot at top speed. There came the second crack of a rifle, but still the Cossack did not pause.

Now Hal, and Chester, dashing after him with Alexis at their side, saw Stephan pause momentarily, raise his rifle and fire quickly twice. Then he dropped to the ground. But it was not from injury, as the others feared, for at that moment there came a volley and bullets whistled overhead. Quickly Hal, Chester and Alexis also flung themselves to the earth.

Stephan, lying upon his stomach, was pumping lead steadily straight before him. Hal, Chester and Alexis drew their revolvers and joined in the fray. Through the trees they could now make out the number of their assailants. There were an even dozen of them, all lying in a little clearing, their rifles trained upon the spot where the four friends lay.

Under the deadly aim of Stephan's rifle, two men dropped to the ground. The others returned the Cossack's fire, but the latter was well protected by foliage, and escaped injury. Another German jumped to his feet, spun round on his heel, and fell to the ground.

Then, at a word from one of the Germans, the remaining nine jumped suddenly to their feet and dashed toward their enemies on a dead run, their rifles spitting fire as they came on. Exposed to the fire of the foe as they were, they realized that their only chance of life lay in rushing their opponents.

Alexis was the first to see the danger in this attack. He jumped to his feet, dragging Hal and Chester with him. Stephan also was up in an instant.

"Quick!" cried Alexis, and at a rapid run, he urged the lads to another secluded spot.

There, as the Germans appeared in the spot where they had stood a few moments before, Stephan, the only one of the four armed with a rifle, fired three more quick shots at the foe. One tumbled forward on his face, and a second dropped his rifle.

And now unexpected aid came to the four friends. From the rear of the Germans came several rifle shots in quick succession, and two more of the enemy bit the dust. As they turned to face this new attack, Stephan stepped forward and opened on them again. Caught thus between two fires, the Germans fought well, firing blindly at their unseen foes on both sides.

But such a struggle could have but one ending. The Cossacks, screened from the fire of the enemy who lay between them, were practically safe from the German fire, at the same time having the Germans at their mercy. No quarter was asked, nor none was given. Soon a heap of fallen bodies marked the spot where the Germans had made their last stand.

From the other side of the Germans, two Cossacks now stepped forth, and approached. Stephan advanced to meet them. Alexis made his way to the fallen foe, and gathered up the rifles. Returning, he passed one to each lad, with the remark:

"Here; these beat revolvers for this kind of warfare."

After a short conference with the two newcomers, Stephan motioned for his friends to follow, and the party, now increased to six, moved on. For perhaps half an hour they marched through the woods, and at the end of that time stopped once more before the entrance to a second cave.

"Before we enter," said Stephan, "I will tell you that these men have just informed me that inside a consultation of war is being held. There are perhaps 60 men there, who have gathered here for that purpose. I have vouched for you, and you will therefore be admitted to the consultation without question."

The others signified that they understood, and Stephan led the way into the cave. Inside, the lads looked quickly around. This cave, they saw, was much greater than the first they had entered. Also it showed signs of human handiwork. Large pillars ran up through the center of it, and beyond the far entrance the lads could see one, then two more compartments.

Sitting about on the floor of the first compartment were more than half a hundred men, talking in low tones. They looked up in surprise at the sight of Hal and Chester, but Alexis they greeted with a nod. The latter stepped forward and greeted them in their native tongue. The lads could not make out all he said, but the looks of suspicion on the faces of some vanished immediately, and they moved a bit to let the newcomers join the circle.

Plainly it was the opinion of most of the men that the guerilla warfare had been carried far enough. Some were in favor of making a last desperate raid upon the enemy before attempting to get back across the Russian border, while others were in favor of attempting to get back immediately.

For an hour the discussion waged and then it was rudely interrupted. The man left to guard the entrance to the cavern rushed in.

"Germans approaching in great force!" he cried.

Immediately all were on their feet, and one man rushed to the narrow entrance. He started through but fell back, a bullet in his head. A second, rifle in hand, also advanced, but Hal, springing quickly to his feet, stopped him.

"Wait!" he cried. "They can pick us off one at a time as we go out. Some other plan will have to be found."

Stephan and Alexis took their stand by the lad's side, and faced the men who would have rushed to certain death.

"The lad is right," said Stephan. "Out the other end of the cave, men, and scatter!"

Rapidly this order was obeyed, and soon none were left in the first compartment but Hal, Chester, Alexis, Stephan and Marquis.

Now Hal also dashed after the others. But the lad was not bent upon flight, leaving his friends to face the enemy alone. Quickly he hurried through the three compartments of the cavern, casting a keen eye here and there. Clear to the far entrance he went, and then turned back. As he made his way along, he stumbled over something and fell heavily. He was up in a moment, however, and glanced curiously at the object over which he had tripped. Then a smile lighted up his face. He made his way back to his friends.

"How many do you suppose there are out there?" asked Alexis.

"We have no means of telling," replied Chester. "However, there are probably no less than two or three hundred."

"If we stand here and fire as they attempt to enter, we may have some success," said Stephan.

"Yes," said Alexis, "but the detonations may occasion the falling in of the cavern. At the first shot from outside a piece of falling rock grazed my shoulder."

"We must do something quickly," said Hal. "We cannot leave without striking at least one blow at them."

"Assuredly not," agreed Alexis. "I have a plan."

CHAPTER X

THE MIGHT OF ALEXIS

"What is it?" demanded all eagerly.

"We will retreat to the second compartment," said the giant, "and I will place myself behind the pillar, which I can see from here." He stooped and picked up a long heavy iron bar from the ground. "I will have this for my weapon, and invisible in the darkness, if they come in a rush, I can let my bar fall upon their skulls thirty times a minute."

"Good!" cried Hal, "and at the same time I have another plan. The rest of us shall retreat to the third compartment, leaving Alexis, for the moment, to deal with the foe alone. But Alexis, when I say retreat, you must leave your post and come to the third compartment. Is it agreed?"

"Agreed!" cried the giant.

"All right, then. To your post!"

Quickly the four retreated to the second compartment, where Alexis took up his post behind the large pillar, concealed from view by the narrowness of the entrance between the compartments themselves. The others retreated to the third compartment.

For a long time, it seemed to Alexis, he waited in silence. Then the head of a man appeared through the entrance to his compartment and came toward him. There were more heads behind him.

"Strike, Alexis!" came Hal's voice from the next compartment.

The giant obeyed. The iron bar rose and fell full upon the head of the first man, who dropped without a cry. Ten times in almost as many seconds the huge iron bar rose and fell again and not once did it fail to find its mark.

The German soldiers could see nothing; they heard sighs and groans; they stumbled over dead bodies, but as they did not realize the cause of all this, they still came forward. So far there had not been a sound to tell those behind what was transpiring in front.

But now an officer, bearing a torch, approached. On arriving at the entrance to the compartment where Alexis had exterminated all that had come, he drew back in terror; but his retreat was blocked by those pressing on from behind. The officer saw the heap of dead, but as yet he had not discerned the cause.

Suddenly a gigantic hand issued from nowhere and clutched him by the throat. A second later the captain fell close to the now extinguished torch, adding another body to the heap of dead. All this was effected as mysteriously as if by magic. Another officer, unable to account for the pile of dead, cried to the men behind him:

"Fire!"

A volley rang out, and for a moment the cavern was lighted as if by day. But none was hit. From behind him Alexis now heard the sound of Hal's voice.

"Come back quickly!" whispered the lad.

The giant obeyed instantly, and glided softly through the door to the third compartment. Hal took him by the arm and led him to the side of the room, where he showed him the object over which he had stumbled when in the compartment a few moments before. It was a barrel of powder.

"Alexis," said Hal, "you will take this barrel, the fuse of which I am going to light, and hurl it at our enemy. Can you do it?"

Alexis stooped over the barrel, weighing fully seventy pounds. He lifted it easily with one hand.

"Light it," he said briefly.

"Throw it right in among them," explained Hal.

"Light it," repeated Alexis.

Hal did so, and the giant, picking up the barrel, advanced to the door of the compartment. Beyond he could hear the confused shouts of many men, as they in vain sought to explain the death of their companions.

Alexis blew on the fuse, that it might burn quicker.

And now, by the light of the sparkling fuse, the enemy made out his form. They saw the barrel he held in his hand; they understood what was going to happen.

A cry of terror arose. Some attempted to fly; officers cried out to Alexis that they would spare him if he would extinguish the fuse. Others commanded their men to fire; but the latter were too terrified to do so.

Now the arm of the giant swung round. There passed through the air the train of fire, like a falling star. The barrel fell into the midst of the terrified German soldiers. Immediately Alexis dashed for the far end of the cavern, just outside which his friends now stood.

Then, from inside the second compartment came the terrible thunder of the explosion, blowing the cavern to pieces, hurling men to death by the force of its shock, falling stones crushing out the life of many more.

Alexis dashed for the open air, where his friends stood awaiting him, a happy smile on his face at the success of his exploit. Three more paces and he would be free of the cavern–two more. And right at the exit, a heavy piece of rock, sent hurling in the air by the explosion, fell upon him–striking him upon the shoulder–bearing him to the ground–pinioning him beneath it.

And at the same instant the walls of the cavern began to give. Chester, realizing what was happening, sprang into the mouth of the cave, closely followed by Hal and Stephan. Now, under the massive rock, Alexis stirred. In spite of the great weight upon him, he turned slowly under it, until it rested squarely upon his back. Then stretching his hands out before him, he rose to his knees balancing the rock upon his back. Then he straightened up, and the rock tumbled from him with a terrible crash. He turned, and with his friends, dashed from the cave.

They had not escaped a second too soon.

There was a terrible rending sound, the crunching of rock against rock, and slowly the walls of the cavern gave; then fell inward with a fearful crash.

Some distance from the cavern the four stopped running. Hal wiped the moisture from his brow.

"A close call and no mistake," he said weakly.

Chester grasped Alexis by the hand.

"I thought you were done for," he exclaimed.

Alexis grinned.

"Can't kill me that way," he said. "What's a little rock like that? It was play for me to lift it."

"Maybe so," replied Chester, "but even now, I can scarcely believe what I saw."

"Why," said Alexis, "I could have lifted that rock with one hand. It was child's play. Now I can still remember one great feat I accomplished. It was in St. Petersburg–Petrograd now, by the grace of God and the Czar. There is a little stream runs through the city. Over this there is a bridge. I was passing along one day, when I saw that the bridge, having been weakened in the middle, was about to fall. Well, there was no one on it, so that would have been all right. But, dashing down the street was an ambulance. The woman in it was very ill. It was absolutely necessary that she be taken across the bridge at once. At the bridge the driver was held up. The guard would not allow the ambulance to cross. It was too dangerous. But delay meant death for the lady. I leaped into a small boat and was quickly under the middle of the bridge. The bridge was low, and by standing I could just touch it. I put my two hands under the bridge and braced it while the ambulance crossed. I was sorely tested, but I held out. I account that one of my greatest feats."

"And so you should," said Hal dryly.

"But," demanded Stephan, who was greatly interested in his brother's wonderful narrative, "how is it, that with all that weight resting upon you, and you standing in a boat, the boat didn't sink? I can't understand how, with that weight upon it, it remained afloat."

"Why," said Alexis with perfect gravity, "I forgot to mention that the stream was very shallow–in fact it could be waded. The boat was forced down by the great weight until it rested on the bottom. In that way, it was perfectly simple."

"I see," exclaimed Stephan. "A wonderful feat, truly!"

"Was the bridge made out of rubber?" asked Chester, laughing to himself.

"Rubber?" repeated Alexis. "No; it was a wooden bridge."

"Then," said Chester, "how do you account for the fact that it stretched so when the boat went to the bottom of the stream?"

"I didn't say it stretched," said Alexis.

"I know you didn't say so," grinned Chester; "but it must have stretched unless it broke in two."

Alexis looked aggrieved.

"If you don't believe me—" he began.

"I wouldn't dispute you for the world," said Chester. "I just wondered."

Alexis would have replied, but at that instant his hat was lifted from his head, and all four became aware of the distant sound of a shot. Quickly all dropped to the ground, but they were not quick enough to go unscathed. A bullet struck Stephan in the arm, and he dropped it to his side with a cry.

Instantly Alexis was all anxiety. He jumped to his brother's side.

"Are you much hurt, Stephan?" he asked tenderly, taking the injured arm in his hand.

"Just a scratch," replied Stephan. "I'll be all right."

Nevertheless Alexis would not rest until he had bound up the wound with his handkerchief. In the meantime, from their positions on the ground, the others had been popping away at the enemy. Several rounds of shots were exchanged but none of the four friends was hit again. The enemy was so far away that the lads could not tell whether or not their fire was effective.

Bullets began to drop closely about them, in their exposed position. Also they fell oftener now, indicating that the force opposed to them was numerically superior.

"Great Scott!" exclaimed Hal, as his hat seemed to leap suddenly from his head. "We'll have to get away from here. This is too close for comfort."

"You bet," said Chester. "Now when I say the word we'll all jump to our feet and make a dash for those trees in the distance."

At the word, the four sprang to their feet, and not even waiting to take a parting shot at the enemy, dashed away as fast as their feet would carry them. Hal took the lead, and behind him came Stephan, then Alexis and then Chester.

When Hal reached the trees, uninjured, he turned to speak to Chester. What was his amazement and dismay to find that Chester was not there. At that moment Alexis and Stephan dashed into the shelter. Hal glanced back over the distance they had come.

There lay Chester, in the open field. He had been struck down by a German bullet, and even now the enemy, with a triumphant cry, was charging down upon him. With a cry, Hal leaped forward, but the iron hand of Alexis stayed him.

"You stay here," said the giant. "I'll get him!"

Discarding his rifle, he dashed forward in the very face of the onrushing foe. Chester's life hung in the balance!

CHAPTER XI

TWO TO THE RESCUE

As friend and foe alike bore down on him, Hal saw Chester raise himself. He got to his knees, struggled to his feet, staggered, and then fell back again.

The Germans rushing toward the lad numbered twenty–Hal counted them. They were approaching the prostrate form of the lad as rapidly as they could, afoot. But Alexis was nearer, and it was evident that he would reach the lad first.

The giant Cossack covered the intervening space with long bounds, going at a speed of which Hal had not deemed him capable.

And now, as he came close to Chester, a second form bounded after him. There was a flash of a hairy body as Marquis leaped forward and set out after Alexis. He came up with the latter before he reached Chester, and they came to the lad's body together.

In the meantime, Hal and Stephan kept up a steady fire with their rifles, pouring a hail of bullets in the direction of the advancing Germans. One man fell, but the others dashed on.

At this point Hal made a startling discovery. The magazine of his weapon was empty and he had not another cartridge. At the same moment Stephan fired his last remaining shot. Hal sprang forward and seized the weapon Alexis had thrown down when he dashed to Chester's aid. It was empty. The lad uttered a cry of dismay, and turned his eyes. The two still had their revolvers, but the distance was too great for a pistol bullet.

Alexis, having reached Chester's side, knelt and raised the lad's head to his knee. Hurriedly he drew his canteen and poured a little water down his throat. Chester looked up into the Cossack's face and smiled feebly. Alexis tried to place him upon his feet, but the lad was too weak to stand.

A fierce growl from Marquis, who had been standing guard over the two, with bared fangs and bristling back, called Alexis to more serious work. The Germans, apparently fearing nothing at the hands of one man, a wounded boy and a dog, had come within fifty feet without firing a shot at the trio. Now, as they approached closer, the leader of the band called out: "You are my prisoners!"

Without waiting to reply, Alexis leaped toward them. His sword flashed from his scabbard and whirled aloft even as he jumped. He was among the enemy before they realized what had happened.

The suddenness of the giant's spring stood him in good stead. Before a rifle or a revolver could be brought to bear on the huge form, Alexis had come to such close quarters with his foes as to prevent the use of firearms. The German leader did draw his revolver, but the mêlée was so fierce and men were tangled up so that he was unable to fire for fear of hitting one of his own men.

To the right, to the left, and straight ahead darted the fiery sword of the giant Cossack. The Germans gave back before the very savageness of this attack, but Alexis kept close in among them, for while he was fighting mad, he was still cool enough to realize that his hope of life lay in his keeping in the center of the enemy.

Before the thrust of the angry sword three men fell. The blades of the others who encircled him hissed above his head, flashed by his side, but his single weapon so far had formed a perfect barrier. Not a thrust or a slash had passed it. Ten swords clashed against the giant's blade at once. With a quick move, he swept them all aside, and with a quick thrust disposed of another of the enemy.

With a rapid spring forward he avoided the weapons that would have been buried in his back by his foes in the rear, and sweeping his sword around his head with such rapidity that he seemed a circle of fire, for a moment he cleared a space around him.

But in that instant the German officer brought his revolver to bear and fired.

Alexis had perceived this move out of the tail of his eye and, leaping straight forward into the midst of the foe once more, escaped the bullet.

Whirling his sword about his head, the Cossack spun on his heel. The guard of the German soldiers was not strong enough to ward off this terrible blow. Two swords went spinning in the air, and Alexis' weapon, sweeping through one of the enemy, also cut down another. But again the Cossack had left an opening for the officer's pistol, and the latter was not slow to take advantage of it.

Slowly he raised his weapon and took careful aim. He had determined not to miss this time. His finger tightened on the trigger, and—

Aid came from an unexpected source.

Marquis, who, up to this instant, had remained alert over Chester, had not taken a hand in the battle. His eyes fastened at this moment on the German officer, his canine intelligence told him as clearly as words that his giant friend stood at death's door. With one fierce growl, he sprang from Chester's side, and leaped upon the German officer from behind, even as the latter pressed the trigger. The officer's aim had been deflected, and the bullet passed over Alexis' head.

The German turned upon this new assailant with an imprecation. His hand went to his holster in an attempt to draw his second revolver. But Marquis was prepared for this move. His teeth met in the officer's hand and the latter yelled with pain.

Marquis released his hold and sprang straight at his enemy's throat. The latter was thrown from his feet by the force of this attack, and in falling his head came in contact with the sharp barrel of his revolver, knocking him unconscious.

Marquis, now having entered the battle, had no thought of leaving Alexis to fight it out alone. Once in the fight, he was there to stay. He sprang forward and leaped upon a German soldier who at that moment would have plunged his sword into Alexis' defenseless back. The man gave a choking cry as the teeth of the dog found lodgment in the back of his neck and he was borne to the ground.

And still the giant Cossack, with herculean strength and unbelievable prowess, was fighting his assailants. A sword had pierced him through the left hand, another had scratched his cheek and a third had struck him in the right shoulder. But still, unmindful of these wounds, he fought on with the same determination and courage as before.

Marquis, having dragged the man off his back, Alexis plunged into the midst of his enemies anew. Two more were pierced through and through by the quick and mighty thrusts of the powerful arm. Another dropped with a bleeding head, as Alexis caught him squarely with a quick back-handed blow just in time to avoid the point of the other's weapon.

Now there were but eight Germans left, and these leaped quickly backward, thinking to put enough distance between them to allow them to draw the revolvers. But Alexis gave them no time for this. Springing after them as they turned to flee, he cut two more down with mighty strokes. Then the

67

others scattered. The Cossack sprang after one and disposed of him before he could draw his pistol, but the others now had had time to get their guns.

A bullet struck Alexis in the right shoulder, but he did not even stagger. He rushed quickly upon one of his enemies, who stood with a revolver pointed squarely at him, his finger on the trigger. There was a sharp report, followed instantly by another and the German fell to the ground with a bullet in his head. Alexis sprang out of the cloud of smoke unharmed.

This time the Cossack had been saved from death by the hand of Chester. The lad having recovered sufficiently to take in the scene about him, had staggered to his feet, thinking to go to the aid of his companion. But he was so weak he could not stand. Then, seeing the revolver dropped by the German officer, he had crawled toward it. At last he reached it, and he had just time to aim and fire before the man who had drawn a bead on Alexis could pull the trigger.

There remained but four Germans on their feet, and these, having witnessed the mighty prowess of the giant Cossack, turned to flee. But Alexis was after them in a flash. His blood was up, and though bleeding in a dozen different places, he had no mind to quit the battle until the last of his enemies had been laid low.

But the fleeing Germans, unfortunately for them, had turned their faces in the wrong direction. Hal and Stephan, who had been struck spellbound by the terrible fighting of their friend and brother, saw the four men coming toward them, weapons in hand, with Alexis in hot pursuit. Quickly they aimed and fired. At this distance a miss was impossible. Two Germans staggered in their stride, reeled, and dropped over backward.

The others halted, appalled by the forgotten presence of this new enemy. The stop was unfortunate for them. Alexis bore down on them like an avenger, and close on his heels came Marquis. The Germans hesitated, then started to run. It was too late.

Alexis' mighty sword cut down one before he had taken a dozen steps. The other, bewildered, and not knowing which way to turn, threw down his weapons and raised his hands in token of surrender.

Alexis, however, did not perceive this move. The light of battle still flashed in his eyes, and he could see nothing but glittering swords and shining revolver muzzles. His upraised sword would have split the head of the German, had not Hal, stepping forward quickly, caught the blow upon his own weapon.

"Alexis!" he cried sharply.

The giant paused and looked around as one in a dream. Then he slowly raised his sword, gazed at the lad blankly for a few seconds, spun twice around and fell forward on his face. He had swooned.

Stephan leaped forward, and from his canteen poured water over the face of his brother. Knowing that the giant was in good hands, Hal dashed forward to where Chester still lay, having fallen back after firing the one shot. The prisoner, now unguarded, took to his heels and was soon out of range.

"Are you badly hurt, Chester?" asked Hal, anxiously, bending over his friend.

"I feel pretty weak," was Chester's reply. "But I don't believe I am seriously hurt. A bullet must have grazed my temple, and the force of the shock put me out. But say! Isn't Alexis a terrible fighter?"

"I should say he is," answered Hal. "I don't believe anyone ever saw such fighting before. Certainly not since the days of Hereward."

Hal assisted Chester to his feet and, supporting him by an encircling arm, led the way to where even now Alexis, having received first aid treatment at the hands of his brother, was sitting up and gazing about somewhat vacantly.

Chester spoke to the big Cossack.

"I owe my life to you," he said simply. "I shall never forget it."

"That's all right," replied Alexis. "I remember now. It was quite a fight, wasn't it? But I remember once when I was attacked by—"

His voice died away, and he sank to the ground again.

His friends bent over him anxiously, and Hal placed a hand over his heart. It was beating regularly while his deep and regular breathing proclaimed his condition.

"He is sleeping," said Hal quietly.

CHAPTER XII

ON THE VISTULA

"How far are we from the Vistula now, Alexis?" asked Chester, as the little party rode rapidly forward.

"Not more than seven or eight versts, I am sure," was the reply.

"Is it likely the Germans have advanced that far in this section?"

"There is no telling; we shall have to be careful."

All day long the four friends had been hurrying toward the Russian lines. Alexis, after his terrible struggle with overwhelming odds, when he had dashed forward to save Chester, had slept for hours without moving-all night, practically. When he awoke, shortly before dawn, he announced that he was in condition to move on.

Chester's wound also had benefited by the rest and now bothered him little. While Alexis and Chester slept, Hal and Stephan had succeeded in capturing four horses; and so, long before sunrise, the little party continued their flight, Marquis, as usual, trailing along behind.

For another hour now the four rode on, and then a welcome sight confronted them. Hal was the first to perceive water ahead, and called the attention of the others to it.

"The Vistula," said Alexis briefly.

There was not the sign of either friend or foe. For some unaccountable reason neither bank of the stream was guarded. Hal supplied an explanation.

"The Germans have probably been pushed back further to the South," he suggested, "thereby doing away with the necessity of a patrol here."

They drew nearer the river. At this point the stream was very deep, and there was no bridge; but as the four drew up on the bank, Chester made out a cloud of smoke coming up the stream.

"A steamer!" he exclaimed.

The lad was right. The smoke drew nearer, and at last the friends were able to discern the outline of a small river vessel steaming toward them. They jumped from their horses, and advanced to the very edge of the water, where they awaited the approaching boat.

"She may be a German," said Hal.

"It is hardly likely," said Alexis.

"But I understood the Germans had fitted out several river steamers," said Hal.

"True," replied Alexis; "I had forgotten. We shall have to be careful."

But now the vessel was close enough for those on shore to make out her flag. The emblem flying aloft was that of the Czar. Hal drew off his coat and waved it about his head.

"If they will stop and pick us up," he explained, "it may save us a tedious ride."

A sharp blast of the whistle signified that Hal's signal had been seen. The steamer came to a stop in midstream, a launch put off toward the shore, and soon grounded at the spot where the four friends stood.

Quickly they leaped into the little craft and were soon aboard the steamer, where they were greeted by the commander of the vessel. Hal explained their situation as briefly as possible.

"Well," said the commander, "I can't promise to put you ashore immediately, for I am bound further up the river in pursuit of a German steamer that has been bombarding several upstream towns. When I have disposed of the enemy, however, I shall be glad to land you down the stream, for I shall return immediately I have sunk the foe."

With this the fugitives had to be content. They were assigned quarters on the steamer, and after washing the dirt and grime from their hands and faces, they returned on deck, where they made themselves comfortable as the steamer continued on her way. They passed several little towns without stopping.

Suddenly those on deck were brought to their feet by the booming of a single heavy gun. All strained their ears to listen. The first report was followed by the sound of others. The commander of the vessel sprang to action.

"Full speed ahead!" he cried.

The steamer leaped forward faster than before. The crew prepared for action. The guns were made ready and the crews stood to their posts. The commander, from his position, motioned the four friends toward him.

"We have run the enemy down," he informed them. "Can I count upon your services if they are needed?"

"You may," replied Hal and Chester briefly.

Alexis and Stephan nodded their heads in assent.

"Good!" said the commander. "You will stay here near me, then. I shall not hesitate to call upon you."

Rounding a slight bend in the river, the Russian steamer came in full sight of the enemy. So silently had she approached, that the Germans, engaged in hurling shells upon a little village, did not perceive their presence until a shell from the Russian plowed up the water under the prow of their boat.

As soon as the Germans became aware of the presence of another enemy they turned to meet it. Their forward guns were quickly trained upon the Russian steamer and burst into action. The first salvo was harmless, for the range had not been gauged accurately.

The Russians were more fortunate with their second fire. A shell burst squarely upon the deck of the German with a loud explosion. There was a shower of steel and wood, followed by a cry of triumph from the crew of the Russian vessel. A second shell carried away the enemy's single smokestack and a third burst in the muzzle of one of the foe's forward guns, blowing it to atoms.

At full speed the Russian advanced, and when within two hundred yards swung her broadside to the enemy and poured in a rain of shells. The Germans fought back gamely, but with the first success of the Russians they seemed to have lost their heads and fired wildly. Their aim was poor, and the Russians suffered little.

Having delivered his broadside, the Russian brought his forward guns to bear and with these he raked the deck of the enemy–fore and aft–with shot and shell.

All this time the vessels had been drawing closer together. Now the German commander, apparently realizing that he was fighting a losing battle, steamed full speed for the Russian ship. By a hasty maneuver the Russian commander avoided being run down, but a second later the vessels crashed broadside to broadside.

The German vessel stood somewhat higher in the water than did the Russian craft, and before any aboard the latter realized what was happening, the foe swarmed down the side onto the Russian vessel. So sudden and unexpected was their onslaught, that for the moment the Russians on deck gave way before them; and had it not been for the presence of mind of Hal and Chester, it is likely the German rush would have been successful.

The two lads sprang forward into the very faces of the enemy, their automatics spitting fire as they leaped. Alexis and Stephan came close behind them. The very fury of their attack caused the Germans to halt momentarily, and this gave the Russian sailors time to rally and spring to their aid.

Their automatics having been emptied, the lads leaped into the thick of their foe, striking out with their naked fists. Hal twisted a sword from the hand of a German officer, and laid about him lustily. Chester, stooping, came to his feet with a sword in his hand, and joined his friend in the press. Alexis also possessed himself of a weapon and rushed forward.

By this time the Russian sailors had met the foe and the conflict became general. Slowly the Germans gave way, retreating to the side of the ship. Then, suddenly, they turned and leaped for their own vessel, which still lay close, under the guiding hand of the German commander. The Russians plunged after them, following them to the deck of the German ship.

Brought to bay, the Germans turned in a last desperate stand. Releasing the helm, the German commander himself sprang into the midst of the struggle. His sword flashed aloft, and two Russian sailors hit the deck, pierced through and through. He was a big man, this German commander, and a powerful one. As he pressed fiercely forward, for a moment the first line of Russians gave way; but at that moment he ran against a solid obstruction in the form of Alexis.

They fell to, hand to hand, and on all sides of them the others gave way. Thrusting and parrying, the two skipped forward and back, each losing ground and then recovering it. Alexis, by a quick sidestep, avoided a fierce thrust, and stepped forward to put an end to the encounter. In his haste he slipped, and slid to the deck.

With a fierce, guttural cry of satisfaction, the German stepped forward, raised his sword and would have plunged it into his opponent's breast; but Alexis was too quick for him. With his bare hand he seized the naked blade aimed at him and clung to it. In vain did the German try to draw his sword through the Cossack's hand. Alexis' mighty grip held it easily.

Now, putting forth greater exertion, by the aid of the weapon to which he clung, Alexis dragged himself to his feet. In vain did the German commander wrench at the sword. He could not free it. He at length gave up the idea, dropped the sword and leaped back.

As Alexis, now firm upon his feet once more, took a step forward, the German commander turned and ran toward a rack of rifles. Alexis did not take time to reverse the weapon he still held by the point. Raising it high above his head, he carefully gauged the distance, and let fly. The sword went hurtling through the air, turning once in its flight. Alexis' aim was true, and the point of the weapon pierced the German commander squarely between the shoulder blades. He threw up his hands and fell forward on his face.

Alexis turned and surveyed the battle.

The Germans had been pressed back by the Russians, led by Hal and Chester, until now they were fighting desperately on the stern of the vessel. Alexis dashed forward to take part in this fray; but the Germans, having witnessed the death of their commander, had lost heart. Perceiving the giant form rushing down upon them, they threw down their arms as one man. Some turned quickly and leaped overboard into the river and struck out for the shore, while others stood quietly waiting to be bound by their captors. The battle was over.

Immediately the commander of the Russian steamer ordered his men and the prisoners back aboard his own ship. Then he turned to Hal and Chester.

"As you have taken such a prominent part in this victory," he said, "I will allow you to finish the work by blowing up the enemy. You will attach a fuse to the magazine and then hurry back here, that we may reach safety before the explosion."

The two lads saluted, and made their way to the magazine of the German vessel. Here they quickly attached a fuse, and lighted it. Then they hurried aboard the Russian steamer, which immediately got under way. One hundred yards, two hundred yards, three hundred, they steamed from the doomed vessel; then there came the sound of a muffled explosion, the German craft burst into a sheet of flame, broke into two pieces, and settled slowly beneath the waters of the Vistula.

"A good job done," said the Russian commander briefly.

He turned once more to the two lads. "I want to say," he added, "that it has never been my fortune to meet two braver lads. You are English, I take it?"

"Americans," replied Hal briefly.

"So? Still, I might have known it. I have known several Americans, and they were always cool and brave. Where do you wish to go now?"

"Well," said Hal, "we would like to get back to Lodz. I suppose our regiment is still stationed there."

"I will see that you get there with all possible dispatch," the commander promised. "I will land you where it will be most convenient for you."

The lads thanked him, and walked across the deck, where they rejoined Alexis and Stephan.

"You would make a pretty good sailor, Alexis," Chester told him.

The Cossack drew himself up and strutted proudly for several moments.

"Of course I would," he said. "It is nothing new to me."

"Nothing new!" exclaimed Hal in some surprise.

"No," replied Alexis.

"You mean you have been a sailor?" demanded Chester.

"Certainly. Of course the commander of this vessel did a fair piece of work a few moments ago; but I could tell him a few things. Why, when I commanded a ship in the battle of—"

"Enough! Enough!" cried Hal, throwing up his hands in protest.

"Do you doubt my word?" demanded Alexis fiercely.

"Not at all," Hal hastened to assure him. "But, Alexis; have you learned yet what 'drawing the long bow' means?"

"No," replied the giant, "are you going to tell me at last?"

"I had about decided to," said Hal slowly; "but after this, never!"

CHAPTER XIII

INTO THE CARPATHIANS

"So," said the Grand Duke Nicholas, "you find that there are adventures to be found in the eastern as well as the western theater of war, eh?"

"Yes, Your Excellency," replied Hal.

"And tell me," continued the Grand Duke, "what do you think of the Cossacks as fighters?"

"From what we have seen," replied Chester, "I should say that there are none better."

"Good!" was the emphatic rejoinder. "There are none better!" and he regarded the lads silently for some moments.

Hal, Chester, Alexis, Stephan and Marquis, after the battle on the Vistula, had returned to Lodz without difficulty. The commander of the Russian river steamer had made it as easy for them as possible. In Lodz they learned that their regiment had been ordered to the front, and had been on their way to join it, when the Grand Duke, inspecting his troops, had come upon them. He immediately had the two lads taken to his quarters, for he was greatly interested in them. Alexis, Stephan and Marquis waited without.

At last the Grand Duke spoke. "I have a mission for you, if you are willing to undertake it," he said.

"Yes, Your Excellency," replied Chester.

"Very good! As you may know, my primary aim, from the beginning of the war, was an invasion of Hungary–the capture first of Budapest and next of Vienna. This necessitates the capture of Cracow, in Galicia, and the forcing of a passage through the Carpathian mountains–a tremendous feat at this time of year. The investment of Cracow is certain. Even now my troops are within a few miles of that stronghold, and I had word this morning that part of it is in flames. Do you follow me?"

"Perfectly, Your Excellency," replied both lads.

"Very well! Now, in some unaccountable manner, my plans have always been anticipated by the Austrians. How or by whom I do not know; but I believe it has been by some of Brunnoi's bandits, who have a stronghold in

77

the Carpathians, but mingle freely with our soldiers. Do you know who Brunnoi is?"

"No, sir," from both the lads.

"Well, Brunnoi is a veritable bandit chief–a man of great cunning and influence, besides being a born gentleman. A Hungarian, and therefore a Slav, he should naturally support the Russian cause. He has a strong following and his men would make first-rate soldiers. We are seeking his support, and so are the Austrians. However, if it is through his spies that my plans are being given to the Austrians I would like to know it. Do I make myself clear?"

"You mean," said Hal, "that you would have us find out just where he stands?"

"Exactly! He has sent me word that he will espouse our cause, but I fear he may be double-dealing. Naturally, therefore, you will keep your identities secret. That is all."

The lads saluted, and turned to depart, but before they could leave the tent a man in civilian garb entered the tent. The Grand Duke greeted him warmly and then called to the lads.

"I wish to introduce you to Count de Reslau," he said. "He, if any man, can give you information that may be of aid to you."

The two lads acknowledged the introduction, and as he recognized the newcomer, Hal started back. The latter smiled.

"I see you remember me," he said pleasantly. "I must apologize for my previous rudeness. I did not then know you were friends of the Grand Duke."

Both lads bowed. Count de Reslau was the man who had laughed at Alexis in a store in Lodz some time before–the man whom the lads believed to be responsible for their being set upon in the street. The count explained the matter to the Grand Duke.

"Well," said the latter, "I am sure these lads bear no malice." To the boys he added: "The count is one of my best friends. Being a Hungarian he has not taken up arms against Hungary, although he is in sympathy with us. I am sure he can aid you."

He then gave the count an idea of the mission the lads were about to undertake, and the count promised to help them in every way possible.

"Your Excellency," said Hal, as they prepared to take leave of the Grand Duke, "have we your permission to take Alexis with us?"

"And who is Alexis?" demanded the Grand Duke.

Chester explained.

"Take him by all means," was the Grand Duke's reply; "and return to me at the earliest possible moment."

The lads saluted and left the tent. Alexis joined them on the outside and the boys told him of the work ahead of them.

"But how about me?" Stephan demanded. "Am I not to go too?"

"No; I am sorry," replied Hal. "The Grand Duke said nothing about you. Besides, three are better than four."

Stephan was greatly disappointed, and showed it plainly. However, he was not a man to complain. He wished them good luck, shook hands all around and set off to rejoin his own regiment.

Suddenly Hal bethought himself of Marquis.

"We can't take him," he said. "He would be in the way. What shall we do with him?"

Alexis bethought himself of a friend in the city who, he was sure, would be glad to look out for the dog while they were away. Accordingly Marquis was taken to this home, where the woman of the house readily agreed to take care of him; but when they came to leave, Marquis wanted to go, too.

"No," said Hal, and he talked to the dog quietly for several minutes, explaining to him the necessity of his remaining behind.

There could be no doubt that the dog understood, for a sorrowful look came over his face. His tail wagged in understanding of his orders, but there was a hurt look in his eyes. However, he did not protest, and when his three friends finally walked away, he stood looking after them regretfully, although making no attempt to follow.

"The first thing," said Hal, "is to procure three good horses."

"Yes," agreed Alexis, "and another to carry food."

"No," answered Hal. "We cannot be bothered with that. We shall have to live off the country."

Alexis made no objection, though it was plain to both lads that the Cossack would have rather made due preparations to care for the inner man. Three strong, wiry Cossack horses having been placed at their command, the three leaped into the saddles and set off through the streets of Lodz at a slow trot.

Darkness was falling when they came to the outskirts of the city, and turned their heads toward the southwest. As far as Cracow the roads were held by Russian troops in force, and the three travelers experienced no difficulties. They did not go close to the beleaguered city, but bore off a bit to the north, just skirting the great Russian army before the Galician stronghold.

Three days and nights they traveled without incident. Their food they purchased at little towns through which they passed, or at farmhouses; and they slept wherever they happened to be when night overtook them. But now that they were drawing close to the Carpathians, Hal decided that the order of things must be reversed.

"In the future we shall travel at night," he said. "We'll do our sleeping in the daytime."

This plan was approved by both Chester and Alexis, so that the morning of the fourth day found them approaching the long line of mountains.

The Carpathian mountains encircle Hungary on three sides, separating it from Germany on the northwest, from Galicia on the northeast and from Turkey on the southeast. At the southern extremity of the range, a branch proceeds in a southerly direction across the Danube to the center of European Turkey, connecting the Carpathian mountains with the great eastern branch of the Alps.

It can readily be seen, therefore, that the Carpathians are much like the Alps–made up of rugged peaks between which are narrow passes. These passes furnish the only means of getting across the mountains.

In their search for Brunnoi, the boys and Alexis were now approaching that part of the mountains which separates Hungary from Galicia, and through which there are but three passes; so that their traveling had to be done slowly and with great care.

"Now, if you will permit me, I shall take the lead," said Alexis. "I have been in these parts before. Besides I have been told of certain landmarks in these foothills which indicate where Brunnoi holds forth–not definitely enough to lead us straight to him; but I have a general idea of the direction."

No objection being offered, Alexis swung into the lead and the horses plunged up a narrow pass into the midst of the wild hills, probably the wildest and most desolate spot in all Europe. Great trees and massive rocks overhung the little pass, making progress extremely difficult. At the top of the first steep incline, the riders allowed their horses to stop and rest. Then they fared on again.

It was nearing daylight when they came upon a small hut, shrouded by trees, through which a dim light twinkled.

"We'll wait here until daylight," said Hal, "and when the occupants of the hut come out we will accost them."

They waited. Daylight came, and with its coming, a man came from the hut. Hal approached him, and addressed him in German. The man looked at him shrewdly, and then answered in the same tongue.

"Yes," he said, "we can spare you something to eat; also your friends. May I ask what you are doing in the mountains?"

"We are trying to make our way to Budapest," replied Hal. "We were captured by the Russians, and escaped. We are not familiar with the ground, however, and have met with difficulties."

"Well," said the man of the hut, "I can set you right. Come."

Over the meal they talked of the war. Finally Chester said:

"Is there any truth in the report that Brunnoi will go over to the Russians?"

"None!" cried the man, striking the table a hard blow with his fist. "I know, because I am one of his men."

"What!" exclaimed Hal, in well simulated surprise, though he had surmised as much.

"Yes," said the man quietly. "Brigands, they have called us. But they will find that when the Russians attempt to cross the Carpathians, as they surely will, we bandits will give as good an account of ourselves as will the trained troops. We love our country just as well as do those who live in Budapest. But tell me, you are not Hungarians nor Austrians, nor even Germans?"

"No," said Hal, thankful that they had been wise enough to discard their uniforms before setting out upon their mission. "We are Americans."

"Ah!" said the man. "I have heard much of them. And you have been fighting with the German army?"

"Yes," said Chester truthfully.

"But this man," said their host, turning to Alexis. "Is he an American also?"

"Yes," replied Hal, and signified for Alexis not to speak, for fear that his accent might betray him.

Their host was evidently satisfied. The meal finished, the man walked with them to the door, and pointed out the direction they were to take. Then he pointed also to the southwest.

"In that direction," he said, "lies the home of Brunnoi. No, there is no truth that he will espouse the Russian cause. Even now he is able to do much harm to their cause. He is with Austria to the last drop of blood in him."

The three took their departure, going in the direction the man had pointed out. But once out of sight, Hal changed the course, and they bore off to the southwest for several hours, looking for a place to secrete themselves for the day.

"We shall have to be very careful," said Chester.

The truth of this statement was proved a moment later. From behind came the sharp crack of a rifle. Chester's hat leaped from his head.

82

CHAPTER XIV

THE BANDIT CHIEF

Hal, Chester and Alexis threw themselves to the ground with a single movement. A second bullet sped harmlessly overhead.

"We didn't come here to fight," Hal whispered to his friends, "so here goes."

He drew a handkerchief from his pocket, and waved it aloft. This was answered by a command in German, from some distance away.

"Stand up; put your hands above your heads and advance."

The three friends did as commanded. Three swarthy-faced men, with leveled revolvers, advanced to meet them. Quickly they searched their prisoners, relieved them of their weapons, and bound their hands securely.

"Forward march," commanded one, poking the muzzle of his weapon into the small of Chester's back.

There was no help for it. The three friends obeyed.

"Where are you taking us?" demanded Hal of one of their captors.

"To Brunnoi!" came the brief response.

"Great Scott!" said Hal to Chester, in English. "We certainly couldn't have got there quicker any other way. You don't suppose he has learned of our mission."

"I don't see how that is possible," replied Chester.

"Nor I; I suppose the thing to do is to try and convince him we are German soldiers, or else come straight out and tell him who we really are and why we are here."

"The latter way might be best," said Chester, thoughtfully. "For Brunnoi after all may not be such a staunch Austrian supporter as our late host would have us believe."

"True," said Hal. "I hadn't thought of that."

After an hour's ride they came to a little clearing in the forest that covered this point of the mountain. Here they were ordered to dismount, and for half a mile proceeded on foot. As they advanced still further the lads made out the mouth of a huge cavern. Into this dark hole their captors pushed them. Down the mouth of the cavern they walked, and then suddenly came to a sharp turn. Ten more paces and they bumped into a solid wall. One of their captors stepped forward and passed his hand over the surface of the smooth rock, and it gave way before him, turning on well-oiled hinges.

"Great Scott!" muttered Chester. "I have read of these things, but I never expected to see one."

The rock fell into place behind them, and the boys saw that they stood in a well-lighted compartment, in which stood a table and chairs. Their guards led them further along, to where they perceived a closed door. On this one of their captors knocked sharply.

"Come in," came a deep voice from beyond the door.

One of the guards opened the heavy wooden door, and stood back, signifying for the prisoners to enter.

The three friends did so. The room was brilliantly lighted. At a large mahogany desk sat a man in a military uniform, though of what country or what his rank the boys could not tell, for they had never seen a similar uniform and the man wore no shoulder straps. The chairs in the room were beautifully upholstered, and pictures were hung about the walls. All this the lads saw at a single glance.

The man at the desk rose and approached them. He bowed slightly, and, after ordering their hands released, indicated three nearby chairs.

"Be seated, if you please," he said politely, at the same time motioning the guards to withdraw.

Hal, Chester and Alexis did as requested. There was now no question of the man's identity in the mind of any. He wore a long white beard and had a pleasant, kindly face.

Hal rose to his feet.

"Are you Brunnoi?" he asked.

Brunnoi bowed.

84

"At your service," he replied. "Now, what can I do for Lieutenants Payne and Crawford, and their Cossack friend?"

The lads started to their feet upon hearing their own names thus upon the lips of a man they did not believe could possibly know them.

"Come, come, gentlemen," said Brunnoi, smiling at their surprise. "You see, many things are known to me. For instance, now, I could even tell you the object of your expedition to these mountains. Is it necessary?"

Hal threw wide his arms with a gesture of dismay.

"I guess it is not necessary," he said quietly.

"Good!" cried Brunnoi, for the first time evincing real interest in the lad. "You are a man after my own heart. You have nothing to gain by subterfuge."

"Well," said Hal slowly. "You know who we are and the object of our mission. What is your answer? Are you Austrian or Russian? Are you a Slav or not?"

Brunnoi jumped to his feet.

"Yes," he replied, "I am a Slav; but I am not one of your down-trodden Russian Slavs. I am a Hungarian, and a Hungarian–a true Hungarian–to-day is an Austrian!"

"Then," said Hal calmly, "our mission is accomplished. We know where you stand. May I ask you a question?"

"Certainly."

"Is it true that you have been able to furnish the Austrian general staff with the Grand Duke Nicholas' plans?"

Brunnoi was silent for some moments, but at length he replied:

"I don't mind answering that question, for you will never repeat my answer to the Grand Duke. Yes, I have furnished the Austrian general staff with important information."

"Well," said Chester, breaking into the conversation, "what are you going to do with us?"

"Why," said Brunnoi, "for the present you shall be kept here as my guests—prisoners, if you prefer. After that—well, it all depends. Should the Russians come, it may be necessary to dispose of you. Therefore, you should be wise and pray for Austrian success."

"Surely you do not mean that you would murder us?" asked Hal.

"I call it by no such name," replied Brunnoi calmly. "Putting away an enemy is not murder."

"Very well," said Chester calmly. "I suppose there is no use talking about it."

"Not the slightest. Come! Follow me, and I shall show you where you will make your home."

The bandit chief arose from his chair and led the way into another compartment. Hal, Chester and Alexis followed him. This room was also fitted up comfortably, though not as pretentiously as the bandit's office. There were several beds in the room.

"You may make yourselves comfortable here," said Brunnoi. "The door will be always locked, but that need not interfere with your comfort."

He bowed and left the room, and the three prisoners heard the key turn in the lock behind him.

"It looks to me as though we are in a bad way this time, all right," said Chester, when they were left alone.

"A bad way is no name for it," replied Hal; "but tell me, Chester, did you notice anything familiar about Brunnoi?"

Chester clapped his hands together.

"By Jove!" he exclaimed. "Now that you mention it, it seems to me I have seen him some place before. But I can't place him."

"Nor I; but I am positive this is not the first time we have met. It is his voice that puzzles me."

In vain the boys racked their brains. Alexis was called into consultation. He also had been impressed by Brunnoi's likeness to some one he had seen before; but he was unable to throw any light upon the resemblance.

"Well," said Chester at length, "I can't place him and that's all there is about it. Nevertheless, I am absolutely certain I have met him some place before to-day."

The door to their prison was now opened and food was placed upon the table in the center of the room. All three were nearly famished, and they fell to with a will.

"Fattening us up for the slaughter," said Chester with a laugh. "However, I guess they won't kill us to-day."

Slowly the hours passed. There was not a single window or opening in the room, and the prisoners could not tell whether it was day or night outside. But now Hal, glancing at his watch, uttered an exclamation of surprise.

"Almost midnight," he said. "Guess we might as well turn in."

Hal and Chester tumbled into the beds, but Alexis continued to sit in his chair, brooding.

"Come on, Alexis, get to bed," Hal called. "What on earth's the matter, anyhow?"

Alexis did not reply, and Hal repeated his question.

"I was just thinking," said the giant, "what a fool I was to let these fellows take my gun away from me without even a struggle. With a good gun apiece, we might be able to get away from here."

"Cheer up," said Hal. "We are not going to be killed. While there is life there is hope. We'll get out of this ticklish situation somehow. Just be patient."

"Patient!" echoed Alexis; "how can a man be patient cooped up in a place like this?"

"Well, it can't be helped now," said Chester. "Come on to bed."

But Alexis was in no mood to turn in. For perhaps another half-hour he sat brooding; then he arose and made a tour of the room. He put his hand on the doorknob and tried it. It was securely locked, and the Cossack had no doubt that it was also bolted on the far side. He rattled the knob angrily, but there was no answer from the outside.

Alexis continued his tour of inspection. He eyed the table speculatively. It was made of oak and while not of great bulk was very heavy–as much as two ordinary men could lift. Alexis picked it up and tested its weight. Then he growled something to himself.

He also tested the chairs and even the bed on which he was to sleep, all the time growling to himself like a dog. Then, his tour of the room completed, he sat down in his chair again. Hal and Chester had been watching him from beneath lowered lids.

Hal raised himself up.

"Find anything?" he asked.

Alexis vouchsafed no reply.

"Great Scott!" cried Chester, sitting up. "Are you going to mope around all night? Come to bed and get a little rest, that you may be fit to meet any emergency should it arise."

"A good idea," growled Alexis to himself, and extinguishing the light, threw himself upon his bed.

CHAPTER XV

GETTING AWAY

All were up long before a guard appeared with breakfast. This they ate leisurely and then sat down to talk their predicament over calmly.

"There must be some way of getting out of here," said Chester.

"Yes," agreed Hal; "and if we are fond of life, I believe we had better get away soon. But what can we do?"

"You leave this to me," growled Alexis. "I have it all figured out and when the time comes, we will go."

"What!" exclaimed Chester. "You have found a way out?"

"Yes," replied the giant briefly.

"Then—" began Chester, but he was interrupted by the sound of a key turning in the lock of the door.

A moment later the smiling face of Brunnoi appeared in the doorway. He entered the room and closed the door behind him.

"I have come to tell you," he said, "that I am going away for possibly a week. You shall be kept here until I return. By that time I will have decided just what to do with you. I am taking most of my men with me, but I have no fear of your getting out of this room."

"We are grateful for your thoughtfulness in letting us know you are going away," said Hal sarcastically. "I am sure we shall miss you."

"I am glad of that," replied Brunnoi. "Your meals will be brought to you at regular intervals. Till I return then."

He waved his hand airily and stepped quickly through the door, closing and locking it behind him. Immediately he had left the room Alexis jumped to his feet. Hal and Chester watched him in surprise.

The giant Cossack walked over to the bed in which he had slept and quickly stripped it of its coverings. Then, when nothing but the bare frame remained he stepped inside of it. Doubling up his huge fist, he drove it into the footboard with tremendous force. There was a splintering crash and it fell in twain. Wrapping his hardly-used knuckles in a cloth he picked up from the floor, he repeated the operation on the headboard–and the bed lay in four pieces on the floor.

Seizing the first portion by one of the heavy legs, he tore at it with his naked fingers, like a dog at a bone; and soon, exerting his tremendous strength, he had stripped it clean. The second of the smaller legs he treated in the same manner, and likewise one of the larger legs at the head. Then, with these three clubs in his hands, he approached the two boys.

"Here is a weapon apiece for you," he said, extending one of the smaller legs to the lads.

Hal and Chester each took the proffered weapons. They were ungainly and heavy, but the lads realized that they were indeed formidable weapons. Alexis stood looking at them with the big leg resting lightly on his right shoulder. It was a massive piece of wood, this third leg, a terrible weapon in the hands of a giant like Alexis.

"Now," said Chester, "we have these weapons, but how are we going to get out of here?"

"Don't let that worry you," replied the giant. "As soon as we are certain the bandit king is well on his way, we'll get out."

An hour they waited–two hours, before Alexis rose slowly to his feet, indicating that the time for action had come. Slowly he approached the door and pressed his great weight against it. It did not budge.

"Surely you are not expecting to get out that way?" said Hal.

Alexis did not deign to reply. Instead he walked over to the table in the center of the room, and with a single movement swept the dishes on to the floor. Then, lifting the heavy table, he raised it above his head, and advanced upon the door.

Once, twice, thrice the stout oak table crashed against the solid door. It gave slightly. The giant struck the door a fourth tremendous blow, and the table burst into a hundred pieces.

"There," said Chester, "I didn't think it would give."

"I was afraid so, too," said Hal.

Alexis said nothing. Instead he approached the door, and pressed against it—testing it. Then he turned, and without exertion, wheeled a second massive bed into position before the door. This he braced with the third bed, so that by straining his hardest, he could not budge them.

"What are you going to do now?" demanded Hal.

"You'll see," replied the giant briefly.

He stepped between the door and the first bed, close to it. Here, bracing himself against the bed, he laid his great hands against the door and pushed. There was a slight cracking noise. Under this terrible force, the door was straining. And still the giant kept up the pressure.

The muscles in the back of his neck stood out like bands of iron. The sinews in his bare arms quivered and seemed about to leap from beneath his skin; and still Alexis struggled with the unyielding door. There came again the sound of cracking; and the giant released the pressure. Even from where they stood, the lads could see the door sway inward into place, thus showing the pressure that had been put against it.

The two lads were lost in admiration of the great strength of Alexis.

"It doesn't seem possible," said Hal, half to himself.

"It isn't possible," declared Chester.

But Alexis did not heed these remarks. Hurling the beds away with fierce kicks, he cleared a space in front of the door. Then he drew back.

"Look!" exclaimed Chester in an awed voice.

Even as he spoke, Alexis drew himself together for a spring. Ten quick steps he took, and then hurled his giant frame against the heavy door. There was a thud as he smashed against it, followed by a great crash of splintering wood, and Alexis, door and all went down in a tangled heap.

Quickly the giant extricated himself and darted back into the room, where he picked up his massive club. Whirling it wildly about his head he shouted to the lads:

"Come on!"

91

Without a moment's delay, surprised as they were, the lads lifted their own weapons, and dashed after the Cossack. Straight out the door of the bandit chief's private room the three ran into the corridor beyond. Sprawling figures sitting idly about gave evidence that the chief had not taken all of his men with him. At the abrupt entrance of Alexis these jumped to their feet, drawing knives and swords.

Alexis was upon them in a trice, Hal and Chester close behind him. Rapidly the huge club of the giant rose and fell, once, twice, thrice–even to five times, and with each crushing blow a man went down with a crushed skull. The others drew back.

The two lads now ranged themselves on either side of Alexis, and together they charged the foe. There was no escape for the bandits, now backed into a corner; but they fought back with a desperation born of despair. Three minutes later there was not a man standing on his feet.

Alexis rested the end of his club upon the ground, and leaning on it, wiped the perspiration from his brow. Then, after a brief rest, he led the way to the entrance to the cavern, barred by the great rock.

"Here," said Chester, "I am afraid, is where we stop. We do not know how to open it."

Alexis pushed the lads aside and examined the rock. Then, without a word, he dropped his club and put his shoulder to the boulder that barred the exit. The first attempt made no impression. Taking a deep breath, the giant tried again. Putting every ounce of his herculean strength into this final effort, he exerted himself to the utmost.

Slowly the huge rock began to move. Slowly it began to swing outward. Then, more rapidly, until, as the catch was released, it swung away back on its hinges. Alexis, unable to recover his balance, fell forward on his face. He was up in a moment, however, and the three darted from the cavern.

For half a mile they sprinted, seeking to put as great a distance as possible between themselves and the cavern before pausing for breath. Then, suddenly, Alexis toppled over on the ground.

Hal dropped to his knees and gently raised the giant's head.

"Quick, Chester! Some water!" he cried.

Chester darted away, and soon returned with water in his cap. This Hal sprinkled over the giant's face. His efforts were rewarded at length. The color slowly returned, and Alexis heaved a deep sigh. Consciousness was returning.

"Poor fellow," said Hal softly. "He has worn himself out."

"Yes," said Chester, "and had we not brought him along, we would still be prisoners in the cavern, with our death only a question of days or hours."

"True," said Hal. "And such strength," he added, "I never saw before."

"Nor do I ever expect to see again," said Chester.

Now Alexis stirred and groaned. Then he sat up.

"What has happened?" he demanded.

"Through your prowess and bravery," Hal made answer, "we have escaped."

Alexis jumped to his feet and patted himself on the chest.

"It is true," he said, "I am a brave man; and I am a strong man, am I not?"

"There can be no question about either," replied Hal.

"Still," continued the giant, "all things considered, that was not such a remarkable feat. Now I remember once—"

Chester interrupted.

"Come," he said, taking Alexis by the arm, "we must get away from here. The story can wait."

Alexis subsided without further words, and the three continued on their way.

"The thing to do now," said Hal, "is to get back to Lodz as quickly as we can. With luck, we should make it in four days."

"Yes," agreed Chester, "we have learned what we set out to learn. There is no use delaying."

The attention of all three was at that moment attracted by the sound of galloping horses, nearby. The hoof beats were coming toward them. Alexis sprang to action.

"We must have horses," he said in a hoarse whisper. "Otherwise we will be weeks getting back. We will take these."

"How?" demanded both lads in a single voice.

"Follow me," commanded the giant.

Breaking into a quick run he hurried along the road to where it curved sharply. Here they could not be seen by the approaching riders until they actually met.

Alexis took his stand in the center of the road, motioning for the boys to take positions, one on each side of the road. Then all stood waiting.

The hoof beats drew nearer, and then the horses came trotting round the bend.

"Only three! Good!" Hal muttered to himself unconsciously.

The riders were right upon Alexis before they realized that their way was blocked. They quickly drew rein and attempted to check their animals; but it was too late. Alexis had two of the horses by the bridles, and pushing them back on their haunches by main strength, succeeded in unseating the riders.

Hal and Chester pounced upon the two unhorsed men, and had their weapons before they could make a move to defend themselves. Alexis, still holding to the two horses, called upon the lads to cover the third rider, who seemed about to make a dash for liberty.

Hal was quick to obey.

"One move," he said quietly, as he pointed his newly-acquired revolver squarely at the third man, "and you are a dead man."

The latter raised his hands above his head. While Hal kept him covered, Chester advanced and relieved him of his weapons. Then he ordered him to dismount.

Alexis now approached with the other two horses, one of which he turned over to Chester. Hal took the third horse.

"We are sorry to be forced to do this," said Hal to the men whose horses they had appropriated, "but necessity knows no law. We need these animals worse than you do; therefore, we take them."

"We are thankful," said one of the men, "that you have spared our lives."

Quickly the three friends leaped into their saddles, and spurred their horses onward.

CHAPTER XVI

ATTACKED

For several hours the friends rode along the narrow mountain pass without incident. They stopped once at a little mountain stream to quench their thirst and to allow their horses to drink. Then they rode on again.

Rounding a sharp turn in the road, they came squarely upon half a dozen riders, all attired in Austrian uniforms. Hal realized their peril and acted upon the instant.

"Quick!" he shouted to his two friends. "Ride them down!"

The Austrians were no less surprised than the three friends at this unexpected encounter; but they also acted quickly. They reined in their horses and drew their swords and revolvers.

But before they had time to bring their revolvers to bear, the two lads and the huge Cossack were upon them, Hal slightly in the lead.

Hal fired one shot as he swept down upon the foe, but there was no time for more. The nine horsemen met with a shock, but the Austrians, being motionless, had the worst of it. The momentum of the horses ridden by the two lads and the Cossack carried them through.

"Ride!" shouted Hal, as they burst through the enemy.

It was no time for fighting if it could be avoided, and the lads realized it. All three put spurs to their horses and dashed down the road, rounding a bend just as the Austrians, having recovered, fired. None was hit.

"This is one time where discretion is the better part of valor," panted Hal to his friends, who were riding close beside him. "We'll run for it."

The Austrians quickly turned their horses and dashed on in pursuit.

Hal, glancing back, saw that the enemy was not gaining, and reported this to his friends. Thus encouraged, they urged their mounts even faster, and before long had drawn out of sight of the pursuers. But at the very moment they seemed to be safe, Chester's horse stumbled and fell, hurling the lad headlong.

Quickly the others drew up and rushed to his assistance. The lad was not badly hurt, and was soon able to stand. Then, from the rear, came the sounds of their pursuers.

"We can't stand here," cried Hal. "Quick, Chester! Into this clump of trees."

Chester did as told and Alexis followed him. Hal, however, seizing the two horses that were standing led them in between the trees. Then he sprang to the side of the fallen animal. Grasping him by the head, he succeeded in getting him to his feet and under cover just before the Austrians came into sight. A minute later the Austrians swept by.

Hal breathed a sigh of relief.

"Pretty close," he said quietly. "Now let's get out of here by the other side."

Leading the two horses they started on. Five minutes later there loomed up through the trees what appeared to be a barn. They advanced toward it. Not a soul was about, but they proceeded cautiously for they did not wish to walk into a trap.

Hal tried the door to the barn. It was locked. Alexis soon remedied this, however. One quick twitch of his wrist and the lock came off. Hal went in, and started back with a cry of surprise.

"What's the matter?" demanded Chester.

"Matter?" repeated Hal. "Look!"

He stepped back and Chester peered over his shoulder.

"Automobiles!" he said in astonishment

It was true. Inside the shed were four large touring cars.

"What on earth can they be doing here, I wonder," said Chester.

"I haven't the faintest idea," replied Hal, "but if we can find any petrol I should say it is a lucky find for us."

He made a rapid inspection of the shed, and stopped at the far end with a low whistle.

"What is it now?" demanded Chester.

"Petrol," replied Hal. "Gallons and gallons of it. Now what do you suppose it is here for?"

"That doesn't concern us," said Chester dryly. "We'll fill up the tank of one of these cars and get away."

Quickly this was done, and the car was run out the door. Chester climbed into the rear seat and motioned for Alexis to follow him. Alexis hesitated.

"I've never been in one of those things," he said slowly. "Now, a horse is all right. I know all about a horse. But I don't know anything about these things."

"Never mind that," said Chester. "Get in here quick. Those Austrians are likely to be back any minute and we must hurry."

Alexis climbed in, plainly not without trepidation, and sank back in one of the comfortable seats. Hal already had taken his place at the wheel, and slowly the large machine moved forward.

"I wonder," said Hal to Chester, "whether we can go down these passes safely."

"Where a machine has gone once, another may go," said Chester calmly. "Besides, if you'll notice, there is a well-defined track ahead of you, and unless I am much mistaken, it goes not toward the road but away from it."

"By Jove!" replied Hal. "You are right. Now I wonder how that happens."

Gradually the car gathered speed, until it was traveling along at a good gait. Hal did not wish to go too fast, for he was not familiar with the roads, and besides, the steep grade also precluded this.

Night fell. Hal stopped the car long enough to light the searchlights.

"They may betray our presence," he said, "but if I don't light them we are likely to go into a ditch."

The car crept along slowly during the night hours, and morning found them still in the mountains. With the coming of dawn, however, Hal put on more speed, and by noon they were once more on the plains of Galicia. Then Hal "let her out."

Suddenly the machine flashed by a body of troops. Hal swerved to one side of the road just in time to avoid running into them. Chester caught a glimpse of their uniforms.

"Russians!" he called to Hal.

"Are you sure?" the latter called back.

"Sure," replied Chester.

Hal reduced the speed of the car.

"In that event I'll slow down," he said.

The car went along now at a more moderate pace; but once again on a road clear of troops, the speed was increased. They made several stops along the route, and it was late the following afternoon when they recognized the familiar minarets of Lodz. Half an hour later the lads were admitted to the presence of the Grand Duke, Alexis remaining outside in the automobile.

Hal made his report to the Grand Duke clearly and concisely.

"I feared as much," said the Russian commander-in-chief, when the lad had finished. "You have done well, however. You will rejoin your regiment as soon as convenient."

At this moment Count de Reslau appeared in the Grand Duke's tent. He did not at first notice the presence of the two lads, and bowed to the Russian commander.

"Your Excellency—" he began.

At that moment his eyes rested on Hal and Chester and a look of surprise and consternation passed over his face.

"You here?" he cried.

Hal and Chester bowed.

"Yes, sir," said the latter quietly.

The Grand Duke turned to the count with a smile.

"And they have successfully performed their mission," he said. "But it is even as I have feared. Brunnoi will support Austria. And what is worse, my plans are being learned by at least one of his agents and sent to the Austrian general staff."

"Impossible!" exclaimed the count, who had now regained his composure. He turned to the two lads. "Certainly," he said, "when I saw you last I did not expect that you would ever return here. It was a hazardous mission the Duke sent you on. Are you sure your information is authentic?"

"Perfectly," replied Hal calmly. "Brunnoi himself was our informer."

"In that case," said the count with a shrug of his shoulders, "you must be right."

He turned, and with a few brief words to the Grand Duke, left the tent. The lads talked for some moments with the Russian commander-in-chief, and then left the tent, informing him that they would join their regiment the following day. Outside, they climbed again into the automobile and Hal drove the car to the house where they had left Marquis.

The dog was overjoyed at seeing his friends again. His tail wagged fiercely and he barked with gladness, insisting upon kissing all three, in spite of their protests.

"Down, Marquis!" cried Hal with a laugh. "Do you want to eat us up. Now what do you say, sir, will you be glad to rejoin your regiment to-morrow?"

"Yes! Yes!" barked Marquis.

"Good!" said Chester. "But we will leave you here while we get something to eat. Then we will come back and get you."

The three left the house, and made their way to the nearest restaurant, where they ordered a sumptuous meal. It had been long days since they had tasted food in plenty, and they ate hungrily. It was almost dark when they left the restaurant and started after Marquis.

As they passed down a side street, five men armed with long knives sprang out upon them. The three friends were caught off their guard by the suddenness of the attack, and in spite of the fact that they drew their swords, for they were again in uniform, their assailants pressed them sorely. A sword thrust pierced Hal in the arm, and his weapon fell to the ground.

He drew his revolver with his left hand, however, and fired point-blank at his adversary. His aim was true, and there was one enemy less.

At the same moment Chester ran his opponent through, and Alexis brought another to the ground. The other two turned and fled.

"I wonder what that was for?" said Chester, brushing himself off.

"I can't imagine why we should have been attacked," declared Hal.

He broke off; for at that moment he espied a figure standing in a nearby doorway; eyeing them evilly. Hal caught Chester by the arm, and pointed to the figure.

"There is the answer," he said quietly.

Chester gazed in the direction indicated. Then, with a sudden cry, both boys dashed toward the doorway.

For the man they saw, with a sneer curving his lips, wore a long, flowing, white beard and a military uniform.

He was Brunnoi, chief of the Hungarian bandits!

CHAPTER XVII

A STRANGE DISCOVERY

Seeing that he was discovered, Brunnoi darted from the doorway and tried to escape. But he was not quick enough. The lads were upon him in an instant, and beneath their weight the bandit chief was hurled to the ground. He struggled fiercely, clawing and scratching like a cat; but Hal and Chester were too much for him.

Brunnoi finally ceased his struggles and lay quietly in the lads' hands. Hal took him by the collar and jerked him to his feet; then, each lad taking an arm, they led their prisoner straight to the Grand Duke's quarters. They were admitted instantly, and pushing their captive before them, they approached the Russian commander-in-chief.

"Whom have you there?" demanded the Grand Duke, looking at the prisoner.

"Brunnoi, sir," replied Hal calmly.

"What!" cried the Grand Duke, springing to his feet. "Is this the bandit chief?"

"It is, sir," replied Chester.

"I am Brunnoi," said the bandit calmly. "You have me. What will you do with me?"

"You shall be shot in the morning!" cried the Grand Duke angrily.

Brunnoi smiled.

"I fear you are mistaken," he said quietly.

The Grand Duke grew very angry.

"You shall be shot at eight o'clock," he said very quietly. "You have already caused me much trouble. I can't afford to let you escape."

He summoned a guard of an officer and ten men, and turned the bandit chief over to them, with orders that he be shot in the morning at eight o'clock.

As Brunnoi was led by the three lads, he smiled at them.

"I will see you later," he said calmly.

The Grand Duke thanked the lads for their important capture, and then, with Alexis, they made their way to the house where Marquis was waiting for them. They were given connecting rooms and were soon in bed.

Tired out they slept heavily. Therefore, while they had expected to arise before eight o'clock, nine found them still sleeping. They were awakened at last, however, by the sounds of a commotion in the adjoining room.

The two lads sat up in bed and listened intently. Heavy footsteps tramped toward their door and it was thrown open with a quick jerk.

Hal and Chester uttered exclamations of surprise. Confronting them, in the doorway, was the smiling face of Brunnoi, who was to have been put to death an hour before. In his hand he held two revolvers, covering the lads.

"You see I have kept my word," he said. "I was not shot."

"How did you escape?" demanded Hal, asking the only question he could think of at that moment.

"Never mind that," replied the bandit. "Get your clothes on quickly, and come with me."

Under the muzzles of the two revolvers, the lads dressed hurriedly. The presence of Alexis in the adjoining room–the giant lying completely covered up by bed clothes–passed unnoticed. But Alexis, beneath his covering, heard what was going on and understood.

"Go out ahead of me," ordered Brunnoi.

He dropped his two revolvers into side pockets, but kept his fingers on the trigger of each.

"One false move and I'll drop you," he said quietly. "Now, march!"

Slowly the lads left the room, and Brunnoi followed them; but hardly had they disappeared through the door, when Alexis bounded out of bed and silently followed.

At the outside door, Brunnoi stepped back to allow his captives to pass out first. For an instant he was off his guard. It was Alexis' opportunity and he leaped suddenly forward.

Brunnoi heard the sound of the giant's footsteps. He turned quickly, and drew his revolvers, but the Cossack's leap was too quick. With a single movement he sent both of the weapons from the bandit's hands, and reached out to seize him.

Brunnoi was as slippery as an eel. He eluded Alexis' grasp and darted through the door. Now without weapons, he took to his heels.

Hal perceived the flying apparition, and reached out a hand to detain him. He clutched the flowing white beard of the bandit chief–and the beard came away in his hand. Brunnoi fled down the steps and made good his escape, Hal being too surprised to move.

Chester and Alexis were equally as astonished.

"Well, what do you think of that?" demanded Chester, in great surprise. "A false beard! But I wonder how he escaped from the firing squad."

"It's too deep for me," Hal admitted. "But we had better report this to the Grand Duke."

Together they made their way to the quarters of the commander-in-chief. The latter listened to their story with interest.

"I have just learned of Brunnoi's escape from the firing squad," he said when they had finished their account of their experience with the bandit chief. "Count de Reslau, being a Hungarian himself, was greatly interested in this Brunnoi. He asked me for a pass to see him, I granted this request. The guards saw the count leave the tent after a few moments' conversation. But when they went in to lead Brunnoi forth to execution, he was gone, and another man was there in his stead. He had exchanged places with Brunnoi."

"Have you perfect confidence in Count de Reslau, Your Excellency?" asked Hal.

"Absolute confidence," replied the Grand Duke. "Why?"

"No particular reason," replied the lad.

At this moment Count de Reslau himself entered the tent.

"I hear Brunnoi has escaped," was his first remark to the Grand Duke.

"Unfortunately, that is true," replied the Russian commander.

"Strange," said the count. "When I talked to him a couple of hours ago he seemed resigned to his fate."

"But," said the Grand Duke, "he paid these lads a visit soon after his escape. Following a struggle, he again got away."

The count glanced at the lads incredulously.

"Has it ever occurred to Your Excellency," he said quietly, "that these two lads may know more about Brunnoi than they care to admit?"

"What!" exclaimed the Grand Duke.

Hal took a quick step forward.

"What do you mean by that?" he asked calmly.

"You know what I mean," replied the count with a sneer.

He turned again to the Grand Duke. "Has it never occurred to you, Your Excellency, that these boys may be associated with the bandit–that they may have been leading you on."

"But, but," stammered the Grand Duke, "their mission to the Carpathians. Their struggle to get away and their flight. What of those?"

"Mere fiction, I should say," said the count with a shrug of his shoulders.

Hal stepped directly in front of the count.

"That is a lie," he said quietly.

The count raised a hand as if to strike him, then thought better of it and turned away without a word. Plainly the count's words had made an impression upon the Grand Duke. He looked at the two lads closely.

"What have you to say to that charge?" he demanded.

"Nothing," replied Chester, "except that it is too absurd to be given credence."

"Absurd," sneered the count. "You brought the bandit here in the first place, realizing that it would give you standing with the Grand Duke, and knowing all the time that the way had been paved for his escape. If you had no hand in his escape, how did you know he had gotten away before coming here?"

"He came after us," said Hal, "and would have led us away had it not been for Alexis."

"Absurd," said the count again and turned to the Grand Duke. "You see," he said, "how foolish that is. You should have concocted a better story," he added to Hal.

Now the Count de Reslau was one of the Grand Duke's closest friends, and, as the Duke had said, he had implicit confidence in him. It was only natural, therefore, that he should be impressed with his reasoning.

He advanced upon the two lads, and pointed an accusing finger at each.

"The count is right!" he exclaimed in a loud voice. "I can see it all! You are traitors! I would have sworn by your honor in spite of the short time I have known you. You have rendered me, I still believe, valuable service; but you have caused me to play into the hands of the enemy in other matters."

"Your Excellency," said Chester, stepping forward. "Count de Reslau possibly means well, but he is badly mistaken. His reasoning is at fault. We are innocent of this charge."

"You deny it?" fairly shouted the Duke.

"Of course they deny it," said the count. "It is hardly probable they would admit being traitors and spies."

"I understand perfectly," declared Nicholas as he stepped to the door of his tent.

"Orderly," he called, "summon the corporal and ten men."

He stepped back into the tent and turned upon the two lads angrily.

"You shall see how we treat traitors in Russia," he said.

106

An officer and ten men now strode into the tent. The Grand Duke waved his hands toward the two lads.

"Take them out and shoot them immediately."

The officer advanced toward the lads.

"Your Excellency!" exclaimed Hal, stepping forward.

"Enough!" cried the Grand Duke. "I will be trifled with no longer. Officer, do your duty!"

The guards surrounded the boys, and they were marched from the tent.

Count de Reslau smiled to himself as they were led away, and turned to the Grand Duke.

"Let us go out and watch the proceedings," he said.

"Very well," agreed the Grand Duke, and they hurried after the firing squad and the prisoners.

The lads stood facing their would-be executioners when the Grand Duke and Count de Reslau appeared. At that moment, Hal felt something in his pocket that gave him a sudden thrill.

"I am going to take one last chance," he said to Chester. To the Duke he called: "Your Excellency, may I make a last request?"

The Grand Duke nodded an assent.

"I would say once more, Your Excellency," said Hal, "that we are innocent. But," he paused, "I can produce Brunnoi himself!"

CHAPTER XVIII

THE MYSTERY CLEARED

Chester stared in astonishment at his friend. Had he gone mad and taken this means of staying their execution?

The Grand Duke staggered back a step, and Count de Reslau smiled incredulously.

"Have I your permission to do so, Your Excellency?" asked Hal.

The Grand Duke waved his hand.

"You shall have three minutes to produce him," he said angrily.

"Good!" said Hal. "It will require even less."

His right hand was in his pocket. Suddenly it flashed forth, and with it something white. Straight toward Count de Reslau the lad sprang, and before the latter could leap out of the way Hal grasped him firmly by the back of the neck with his left hand, and with his right clapped a long, flowing white beard to his face. Then with a twist, he whirled him so that he faced the Grand Duke.

"Behold Brunnoi, chief of the bandits!" he cried.

The Grand Duke staggered back again, and put one hand to his eyes.

"Impossible!" he exclaimed.

But he was forced to believe what his eyes saw. Count de Reslau and Brunnoi, the bandit chief, were one and the same man. There could be no doubt of that.

In vain did the bandit struggle to free himself from Hal's firm grasp. The lad clung to him tightly in spite of all his efforts. Then, realizing that the Grand Duke must be convinced, he dropped the beard to the ground and stepped back while half a dozen rifles covered the count.

The Grand Duke, with a wave of his arm, instructed the officer in command of the firing squad to release the two lads. Then he ordered him to conduct the bandit chief to his quarters, and motioned the lads to follow. Inside the tent the Grand Duke turned upon his false friend.

108

"De Reslau," he said, addressing the prisoner, "we have been friends, and for that reason I am offering you a chance to make a satisfactory explanation–if you can."

"I have nothing to say," replied the prisoner.

"Will you tell me how you have conducted your operations?"

The bandit did not reply and Hal stepped forward.

"Your Excellency," he said, "I believe I can rehearse it from beginning to end. The count probably will correct me if I am wrong."

The Grand Duke ordered him to proceed.

"Well," said Hal, "the count knew of our mission. We went horseback, but the count, being prepared for these rapid journeys, proceeded by automobile."

The bandit chief glanced at the lad in surprise.

"How did you know that?" he demanded.

"We stumbled upon your automobile garage in the mountains," said Hal quietly. "Of course, when we returned, the count was waiting for us. Why he left us behind alive when he came back here, I don't know, but I now remember how greatly surprised the count was to see us back safely. Immediately he planned to get us out of the way. Hence the attack the other night, in which we were fortunate enough to capture him."

"But the escape?" demanded the Grand Duke. "How did he escape?"

"Very simple," replied Hal. "The man to whom you gave the pass to see the prisoner was of course not Count de Reslau, but a man made up to resemble him. Am I right, count?"

"Yes," replied the bandit. "I have kept him near me for that very purpose. He had his orders that in the event I was ever arrested, he would make up to resemble me."

"Exactly," continued Hal. "Once alone with the prisoner the rest was easy. He removed his disguise, and Brunnoi removed his. Brunnoi came out as Count de Reslau, and the other man stayed. Naturally, the first thing the count thought of when he was free was to dispose of Chester and myself.

109

Hence his call this morning. As he escaped from Alexis I succeeded in pulling off his beard. That's all there is to it."

"And now," demanded the bandit chief, "what are you going to do with me?"

"There is but one thing I can do with you," replied the Grand Duke. "The fate of Count de Reslau shall be the same as that already pronounced for Brunnoi, the bandit. You shall be shot within the hour. Personal friendship shall not keep me from doing my duty. Officer, see that my command is carried out."

The guard closed in about Count de Reslau and he was led away. Then the Grand Duke Nicholas, commander-in-chief of the Russian armies, sank into a chair, and buried his face in his arms on the table. Quietly the lads left the tent.

"By Jove!" exclaimed Chester, as they walked along, "you spotted de Reslau just in time. Another moment and it would have been too late. Tell me, how did you happen to hit it?"

"Ever since I pulled Brunnoi's beard off this morning," replied Hal, "another face has kept flashing into my mind. I could not make it out clearly until just as we stood before the firing squad. Then I saw it as plain as day."

"It's lucky for us that you did," said Chester with enthusiasm. "But here comes Alexis. He'll be glad to know that Brunnoi has been disposed of."

And he was.

"But you make much over a small matter," he said.

"Small matter!" exclaimed Chester. "I should say that proving Brunnoi and Count de Reslau were one and the same person was quite a big matter."

"If you had asked me," returned Alexis calmly, "I could have told you that several days ago."

"You could?" cried both lads in a single voice.

"Of course. I knew it right along. You see, my eyes are unusually keen. I remember once how this keen sight proved of great advantage. We were on a raid. The officer in command, using his glasses, could not quite make out objects moving some miles away. He called upon me. My eyes, being far more powerful than the glass, showed me plainly what was going on, and we were thus kept from falling into a trap. Then I remember another case—"

"One is enough," said Hal dryly. "If you knew Brunnoi and Count de Reslau were the same person, why didn't you say so?"

"Why," said Alexis in no wise disconcerted, "I didn't see that it made any difference."

"Then your sight is not so good after all," said Chester. "But what are we going to do now, Hal?"

"Well," said Hal, "I guess we might as well go get Marquis and return to our regiment. Our work here is done."

The dog was indeed glad to accompany his three friends forth once more, and so, procuring three fiery chargers, the trio set out to rejoin their regiment at the front—some miles to the west of the city of Lodz.

Most of the officers of the regiment to which the three were attached had been killed in the previous battle, and so when they finally reached it, Alexis found that instead of being a lieutenant he had become a captain.

"You see," he told the boys confidentially, "a brave man always comes into his own. You will see how these fellows fight with me at their head. They will be a whole lot different, I can tell you."

The Russians had intrenched themselves along the entire front, as had the Germans only a short distance away. During the days in which the lads had been in the midst of the Carpathians, there had been only skirmishing between the opposing forces. Long range artillery duels raged incessantly; but there had been little work for the cavalry and infantry.

There had of course been several charges and counter charges, but the advantage rested with neither side. The Russian troops, in spite of the cold weather, made themselves comfortable in the trenches, wrapped to the chin in their heavy sheepskin garments. Used to severe winter weather, the Russian troops did not fare as badly as did the Germans, who suffered severely.

The lads' regiment was stationed near the center of the long line of battle. Preparations for a movement of some sort were being made on all sides. Troops were being hurried here and there, and officers dashed hither and yon. Occasionally the men burst into song; while from the German trenches came the chanting of the "Watch on the Rhine." The men of both armies were making the best of the situation, and seemed reasonably happy.

From his pocket one of the Russian officers now produced a pack of cards. Alexis, invited to take a hand, consented, but Hal and Chester refused.

"What's the matter?" demanded the officer. "Are you too good to play cards?"

"Not a bit," smiled Hal. "We simply don't care to play, that's all. We do play occasionally, for pastime, but we don't gamble."

"Don't gamble!" exclaimed the officer. "How can you play cards if you don't gamble. Come on now, we need two more players."

"No," said Hal, decidedly. "We shall have to ask you to excuse us."

Even Alexis glanced at the lads in astonishment. Plainly this was beyond his comprehension, as gambling among the Cossacks is an ordinary pastime. But the other officer was not satisfied. He arose and came directly up to Hal.

"You must play with us," he said.

"I am sorry," replied Hal, "but we do not care to play."

"Afraid, eh?" said the Russian.

"No," replied Hal, "we are not afraid. We simply don't care to play."

"You are cowards," said the Russian, and jostled Hal with his shoulder.

Hal stood his ground and refused to be pushed aside. The Russian reached out a thumb and finger and pulled Hal's nose. Then he staggered back, for Hal had sent his fist crashing against his chest.

Quickly the Russian officer drew his sword and sprang upon the lad, who also drew his weapon and stood on guard. But now Alexis leaped to his feet, and his own sword struck up the weapons of the others.

"Enough of this," he said sternly. "Put up your swords."

"I have no desire to fight," replied Hal calmly.

"I know you haven't," sneered the Russian. "You are afraid. But I demand satisfaction for that blow."

112

"Well," said Alexis, "if you must fight, let it be with fists."

"Any way suits me," said the Russian.

"If he insists on a fight, I am willing to give it to him," said Hal, and quickly threw off his coat.

The Russian also discarded his heavy coat, and the two squared off. It was perfectly plain to Hal that the Russian, although considerably larger than himself, was no boxer, and he had little doubt of the outcome, for the lad was proficient in the use of his fists.

The Russian came forward with a rush. Hal sidestepped neatly, and the huge fist passed by harmlessly. Hal sent a quick sharp blow to the Russian's cheek, staggering him a bit. The latter turned and again rushed at the lad.

Quite a crowd had now collected around the combatants and watched the contest eagerly. As the Russian rushed at him this time, Hal struck up the blow with his left forearm, and stepping in close planted his right over his opponent's heart. The Russian staggered back, and at the same time Hal sent a series of left and right jabs to his opponent's face.

But the Russian, recovering, bored in again, striking out wildly at the lad. The latter gave a clever exhibition of footwork, and not a single blow landed. At the same time he continued to tap the Russian lightly on either side of the face.

Suddenly the Russian lowered his hands and stepped back.

"I quit," he said, smiling foolishly. "There is no use trying to hit a man when he runs away all the time. Now with swords or pistols—"

"There will be no swords or pistols used while I am here to prevent it," exclaimed Alexis.

At that very instant the clear call of a bugle sounded in the Russian trenches. Quickly all personal animosities were forgotten, and the men sprang to their posts.

It was the signal for an advance.

CHAPTER XIX

THE ATTACK

The reconnoitering cavalry of the advancing forces gave way to groups of infantry, scattered in loose formation, feeling their way toward the German trenches. The points and small flanking parties of the advance guards, in front of each column of advance, crept along with straining eyes in search of the enemy's line of observation.

A few hundred yards to the rearward the supports advanced alertly, ready to scatter into a thin line of skirmishers at the first shot and rush ahead to where the points halted. In the rear of them the infantry columns, with one rumble of artillery close to the front, moved and halted, as the thin line to the front paused for a moment to scan ahead, then pushed on again.

Out of the stillness of the dew-dripping woods in front, the shot came. There was no reply for a moment, then two or three closer reports rang loud in reply; then there came another pause, and as the hurrying supports deployed and flung themselves behind the nearest cover, in momentary scanning before pushing ahead to investigate decisively, there came a short, ragged volley from out ahead.

The reports were flat and dull, as a rule, but a few cracked viciously as though fired close at hand. These last followed the vacuum of low-flying bullets and had a spat and twang of their own.

For weeks these two armies had been facing each other; for a week assault had wrestled with counter assault and the armies had striven time after time to snatch an advantage from a massing of columns, or a seeming check.

For miles to right and left, every road, every footpath, every few yards of broken ground was trodden by the feet of short columns, prepared to charge into lines at the needed moment, when the fire of the enemy became a menace. The trenches were abandoned in the rear, yet should the columns in the rear, which by the heads formed a long, long line of supports, be hurled back in repulse after an unsuccessful attack, the trenches would be greeted as comfortable old friends and reoccupied.

The leading columns deployed into thin lines, with short intervals between the men, as the shrapnel broke. From out the blur of the mingling of landscape and sky there came, simultaneously, a whir, a crash, and the quick dash of shrapnel balls over the ground, and of the brief flash which marked the shrapnel's burst there remained only a dimly-seen lingering cloud of dirty smoke and some silent, writhing forms on the ground.

Then came crash after crash, as the hostile artillery opened in strength. The silence of the morning fled into a hideous din as the infantry broke into a dog trot and pushed ahead.

There came a clank of trace chains and the pounding of hoofs mingling with hoarse commands as the artillery of the Russians wheeled out of column to position in battery, the ring of hastily-opened breechblocks, the hollow thump of the blocks closing and the shrill notes of a silvery whistle. Then the earth began to tremble.

Thunderbolt after thunderbolt seemed to be discharging close in the rear, until the very trees shook and men swayed under the compression of air in the vicinity. Over the heads of the silent infantry, shrapnel shrieked in reply, one after another, as the batteries opened with salvos from flank to flank.

Through the gaps between the belching batteries poured the infantry, the columns dashing forward until, beneath the trajectory of the guns, it was safe to spread out in the always thin line of the infantry advance. The leading lines pushed on till they disappeared in the yet dim light, and at a short distance behind them came others, until it seemed that the end would never come, and that a hurrying city was passing.

Ahead, the leading infantry line, absorbing the scattered men of the first light contact line, halted at command under the mounting rifle fire of the enemy, halted and flung itself prone, while ready hands reached backward for intrenching tools, and the line scraped, clawed, scooped and burrowed into the fresh earth in shallow pits, and went about its business of returning the German fire.

Then a second thin line ran up and merged with the first. Again shovel and small mattock came into play and the volume of fire redoubled. Above the cracking of the rifles the only sounds to be heard were the sharp whistles of the officers. They shrilled in a variety of notes and combinations, yet with an understood speech of their own, for in parts of the line the fire slackened and two or three men left their shelter and crept forward a few paces; or, crouching down low, dashed ahead until the whistles spoke again.

Intrenching tool again; then fire. That was the order of the advance. More men crept or rushed to the new position to dig themselves into the ground and open fire, until the entire line had advanced a few yards under the hostile shots and a new line occupied the shelter trenches recently abandoned.

Here and there lay quiet forms across the path of advance. The hardy bodies in the well-fitting uniforms seemed pitilessly small and their clothing hung in baggy folds. Their comrades passed them by with hardly a glance. The litter sections were far to the rear, for their time was not yet. Duty called for assault, not for succor.

The thunder of the contending batteries continued. Over the hastily carved trenches the hostile shrapnel scorched their way, singing along with a note of wild rage, searching the crevasses and folds of the ground and scoring the earth.

But the Russian infantry still advanced.

Quietly filling the gaps that had grown in the firing line since the attack commenced, the supporting lines came to the front. Each accession of reënforcements seemed to give an added impetus to the forward movement, for upon the arrival of each fresh contingent the line surged ahead like breakers on a coast, and, like the incoming tide, each surge left its mark higher upon the strand.

With a calmness which bespoke experience, despite the light of battle which blazed in their eyes, the new men brought and distributed fresh bandoliers of ammunition to those who had gone before, then took their places alongside to aid in its expenditure. The lines were not straight. They zigzagged a trifle. There was no time for chalk-mark adjustment or inspection, and the moment a panting body struck the ground after a forward rush, the earth began to fly on the spot beneath the chop of the trench-digging tools, and the hot rifles to speak.

Men growled, muttered and shouted. Under the fighting fog that beset each one in its own way, there came snatches of song, humming and whistling. There were those, too, who fought silently, as though deeply wrapped in thought, and there was bickering when a hasty comrade crowded too close for free operation of the flying breechbolts; yet the faces were ever turned to the front, except when they turned to the sky or the earth, and nerveless hands fell sprawling with half-emptied rifles.

Where officers, binoculars in hand, bent hastily to the line, men detached themselves at intervals, and clawing at their belts, seized the wire cutters pendant there and crawled forward. Now and then one of the creeping ones would spring into the air and topple over, but the rest, apparently paying no heed, continued on their way toward where the Germans had erected wire entanglements to hold the stormers under the blast of the enemy's fire.

Ahead, the trenches of the Germans crackled and spat with fury, and even under the ceaseless rain of shrapnel from above the assaulting lines the enemy kept his place. The firing line had thickened until it was a solid mass, one man deep, and in the rear line after line had sprung to its feet and was closing up in support to the crucial assault. At the trenches of the defenders, batteries, with horses falling and being cut away in an instant, dashed to the line, unlimbered and poured in their scattering salutations of zero shrapnel to the men in front.

Came a clank and rattle of bayonets snapped onto the muzzles of the assaulting line; then, with a last frenzied emptying of magazines, the lines sprang to foot, and with hoarse voices screeching at top note, the slender line charged forward.

The trenches were lined with the defenders in an instant. The rifle fire redoubled in intensity and the artillery, which had come up to stem the tide, or assault when the supporting batteries of the attack were compelled to hold their fire for fear of obliterating their own attacking lines, barked at four-second intervals, opening great gaps in the racing line at every discharge.

In rear of the supporting lines of the assault, which were closing up at a dead run, galloped the batteries which were to make a rallying point in case the assault failed, or occupy the trenches, should the defenders be driven out, and the cannoneers clutched the side rails as the pieces swayed and rocked across the rough ground and clustered bodies which strewed the field.

At the crest of the parapet the lines, attack and defense met with a ring of steel. Bayonets flashed, darted, parried and struck. Rifle butts whirled above bare heads and the stocks crashed down through bone and flesh. From both sides came a rain of hand grenades, bombs which exploded upon touch. From the rear of the trenches there came running formed troops, to assist in the repulse of the Russians, and as the supporting lines of the attack threw themselves into the fray, the whirling, struggling, fighting lines on the trenches' top thickened and swayed.

The line sagged, bulged, trembled, and broke in huge gaps. Into the splaying breaches there rushed fresh troops from front and rear, and the lines thickened and swayed again. Men discarded their arms to lock in one another's embrace, fighting to the last.

The din was deafening, yet above it there rang out the detonation and shock of a great explosion, where a delayed mine belched upward under the pressure of the hastening troops coming up with the attacking reserve. Earth, stones, wire entanglements, arms and men shot upward in a dense geyser of death, and came down in the midst of the fierce fighting.

Then the line broke again, and the shattered reserves of the attack, summoning the last resources, poured into the breach with bayonet and magazine.

The defense gave way.

Crumpled under the last despairing hurling of last reserves, the entrenched line shuddered along its length, then the line lost its cohesion, stood irresolute for a moment, then fled precipitately to the rear.

The whistles of the Russian officers blew again and again. Officers had fallen until corporals and sergeants commanded platoons and companies; yet they, too, had their whistles and knew their duties; and out of the scramble of the attack, regardless of company, regiment or brigade, the Russians fell into rough line, knelt, and opened fire upon the routed enemy, while the supporting batteries dashed to the trenches, unlimbered and belched fire and iron into the fleeing mass.

The standards of the Russians, which had changed hands a dozen times, during the course of the assault, were planted on the works; the troops themselves, exhausted and spent by the might and fury of their efforts, threw themselves into tired heaps as other brigades came up to hold the position.

The trenches were won!

CHAPTER XX

THE DEATH OF A FRIEND

Hal, Chester and Alexis had been in the midst of the fray, where the fighting was the thickest. Not in the first line of attack, they had advanced with the first reserves. And beside them, snapping, biting and snarling, strode Marquis.

Now the herculean prowess of the giant Cossack stood them all in good stead. More than once Hal or Chester would have gone down, or been trampled under foot by the troops behind, had not the quick eye of Alexis signaled out their danger and his powerful arm come to their aid. Guarding himself perfectly from the sword and bayonet thrusts of the enemy, after the fighting became hand to hand, the Cossack fought like a madman, as did others of his race, hurling himself upon his foes with almost superhuman ferocity.

For the first time the two lads had the experience of digging trenches as they advanced upon the enemy, and in spite of the fact that they were officers, they did not shirk the work. Just before reaching the parapet, the first line of reserves–to which the friends were attached–joined the original first line and sprang into the trenches together.

There they fought with desperation. Not a word was exchanged between them, although they fought side by side. There was no time for conversation. The press was too thick, and death too near.

But now that the Germans had turned to flee, the Russians sent up a wild cry of triumph. Hal, Chester and Alexis rested upon their weapons, watching the troops pour a hail of lead into the flying foe. Marquis advanced several paces ahead of the farthest Russian troops, stood up on his hind legs and let out a bark of joy. Bullets flew around him, and Chester, realizing the dog's danger, whistled sharply. Marquis turned and wagged his tail at his friend, and opened his mouth in one more joyful bark.

It was at that moment that a German bullet struck him. Without a sound the noble animal crumpled up and fell to the ground. The ball had pierced his throat. But life was not extinct. Marquis struggled to his feet, and dragged himself toward Hal and Chester, who, having seen him fall, dashed toward him.

Gently Chester lifted Marquis' heavy weight up in his arms, holding him so that the blood would not flow so rapidly from the gaping wound in his

119

throat. Marquis looked up into the lad's face, and uttered a low, painful bark. His tail wagged.

Quickly the lads hurried back to Alexis and as quickly sought out a surgeon. Chester laid Marquis gently on the ground, and the surgeon bent over him. After a brief examination he arose and shook his head.

"No hope," he said quietly. "The bullet pierced his jugular vein."

"Isn't there something you can do?" pleaded Chester, tears streaming down his face.

The surgeon shook his head sadly.

"Nothing," he said, and hurried away.

Chester picked Marquis up again, and followed by Hal and Alexis, made his way toward the rear, where the troops were more scattered, and where there was none to bother them. Hal drew off his coat, and Chester laid the dog on it.

Marquis did not whimper. He, as well as his three friends, seemed to know that death was not far off, and he was prepared to meet the end bravely, as a soldier-dog should. He turned slightly and licked Chester's hand that lay upon his head. Chester patted him gently, but he was beyond words.

Alexis extended a huge hand and softly stroked the dog's soft body.

"Poor fellow!" he said to himself.

Marquis' keen ears caught these words, and he turned feebly toward the giant Cossack, and strained slightly toward him. At the same time he slowly raised a paw. Chester saw the movement.

"He wants to shake hands with you, Alexis," he said brokenly.

The giant drew nearer, and gravely took Marquis' right paw in his great hand. Once, twice, three times he shook it gently, then laid it upon the ground and turned away. Marquis moved restlessly, and uttered a short bark. He was trying to see Hal, who was kneeling behind him.

Hal arose and came around. To him also Marquis extended his paw, and Hal grasped it and pressed it. Then, shifting his position slightly, the dog also extended the paw to Chester. He seemed to know well that the end was swiftly approaching, and he wished to shake hands with all his friends before he passed away.

Now the three gathered about the head of their dying friend. Alexis clenched his great fists and spoke to Marquis.

"I shall see that you are avenged," he said fiercely. "Twenty German lives will not pay for this day's work, but I'll do the best I can. Do you understand, Marquis?"

Marquis' tail beat a weak tattoo upon the ground, and he barked feebly. He understood.

"I'll do it!" said Alexis. "You may rest assured of that."

Now the end was fast approaching. Marquis' breath came in quick gasps. Suddenly he staggered to his feet, stood upright a second, turned his face toward the distant enemy, and gave utterance to one sharp bark—a bark of defiance. Then he sank to the ground.

His three friends dropped to their knees and bent over him. He looked up into their faces and it seemed to all that he smiled at them. His tail struck the ground feebly, once, twice. He shook once with a silent convulsion. Then his body straightened out and stiffened. He lay still.

Marquis was dead.

His three friends rose slowly to their feet, and lifted their caps from their heads.

"Good old Marquis!" said Hal. "But he died as a soldier should!"

"Yes," said Chester, "and with almost his last breath he breathed defiance to the Germans, whom he hated."

"There wasn't a better or braver soldier in the Russian army," said Alexis. "We must bury him with honors."

"We shall!" cried Chester.

"I am somewhat handy with a knife," said Alexis. "I shall carve him a little monument."

"And he shall be laid to rest with full military honors," said Chester.

And so it was done.

All that day Alexis worked upon the little monument. When it was finally completed, all was in readiness for the burial. The dog had made friends in the regiment. Not a man but had become attached to him; and so it was no small funeral cortege that escorted the body of the dog-hero to his last resting place.

From the quartermaster Chester had secured a large French flag.

"He shall be buried beneath his own flag," he said, and spreading the tricolor upon the ground, he laid the stiffened body of Marquis upon it.

Gently he wrapped it about the dog, and then, while practically the whole regiment stood at attention around the little grave, he placed the body in the ground and stepped back. A volley was fired over the grave, and the lads shoveled in the earth.

Now Alexis approached, and, making a small hole at the head of the grave, set up the little monument. And when he had finished, the soldiers crowded around to read the epitaph that the giant Cossack had inscribed in the hard wood. It was this:

"Marquis–killed on the field of honor!"

It was upon the following day that the welcome news came that there was to be further action. Practically every Cossack regiment at the front in Poland was ordered back to Lodz, their places being taken by other Russian cavalry and infantry.

Again in Lodz the lads learned what this new movement meant. Grand Duke Nicholas, the investment of Galicia having been successful, had decided upon an immediate invasion of Hungary. The Cossacks had been called to lead the dash over the Carpathians into the heart of the enemy's territory.

Hal and Chester had an audience of the Grand Duke. The latter summoned them to his quarters to offer an apology for his hasty action in ordering them shot some days before. Also he talked a little of the proposed invasion.

"Sixty thousand Cossack cavalry will be the advance guard," he informed them. "Behind these will come the infantry in great force. I plan to have a million men in Hungary within two months. If we are successful in forcing a passage of the mountains, and I am sure we shall be, Budapest will be at our mercy, with Vienna as the next goal.

"In the meantime the Poland campaign will be pressed, that the Germans may be unable to go to the aid of the Austrians in the south. The thing that I fear now is that Turkey may be drawn into the war on the side of the German emperor. The Kaiser has brought great pressure to bear upon them, and I fear that they cannot long be kept neutral."

"What effect would that have upon the invasion of Hungary?" questioned Chester.

"It would unquestionably delay it for days, possibly weeks. While we are prepared for the Turks, nevertheless it would probably necessitate the sending of reënforcements toward the border, and naturally I should have to draw upon the forces I am now sending into Hungary."

"I see," replied Chester. "But the Turk, as a fighting man, doesn't amount to much, as I understand it."

"In the recent Balkan war they did not show much fighting prowess, it is true," said the Grand Duke, "but officered by Germans, and under German discipline, there may be a different story to tell."

"But there is no danger of their affecting the ultimate outcome of the war?" asked Hal.

"None," was the confident reply. "What it will mean, however, is that Turkey, as a nation, will be wiped off the map of Europe, and, possibly, of Asia also."

"The sooner the better," was Hal's comment.

The Grand Duke smiled.

"It may take time," he said, "but it will be done just so surely as Turkey casts in her fortunes with Germany."

After some further talk the lads left the Grand Duke's tent, and rejoined their regiment. Everything was now practically ready for the advance to the southward, and the troops were eagerly awaiting the word that was to send them into the Carpathians, to strike a decisive blow at the Austrians.

And the word was given early the following morning.

CHAPTER XXI

RAIDING

At a fierce gallop the troop of Cossacks bore down upon the little mountain town–firing at a detachment of Austrian soldiers who ventured forth to give them battle–without checking their speed. This band of Cossacks, reconnoitering well ahead of the main advance guard, was probably 1,000 strong; the Austrians opposing them much less. With the rapidly advancing Russians were Hal, Chester and Alexis.

The advance of the Czar's troops to the Carpathians had been without incident. Whenever troops of the enemy had opposed them they had been put to flight without difficulty. The cavalry, dashing rapidly ahead, had outdistanced their cavalry and artillery support, and the entire force of mounted men–60,000 of them–were in the midst of the wild mountains.

Harassed from front and, now that they had advanced well into the mountains, also from the sides and rear, the Cossacks nevertheless pushed on. From behind rocks and trees, isolated bands of Austrians fired upon them, doing great execution, disappearing in the hills when the Cossacks turned upon them.

The reconnoitering force to which the lads were attached dashed down upon the little mountain town, the sun gleaming on their lances and revolver barrels. In vain did the Austrian officers urge their men to stand firm. After one volley at the approaching horsemen, they broke and fled, scattering in all directions. The very name, Cossack, spread terror.

Right into the middle of the little village dashed the troop. Now from every window came a hail of lead, and the Cossacks, apparently trapped, turned this way and that, not knowing which way to go. Struck by a rifle bullet, the officer in command threw up his hands and toppled from his horse. Quickly Alexis sprang to the head of the men, Hal and Chester beside him.

"Dismount!" cried Alexis.

The cavalrymen threw themselves from their horses, and at a second command, rushed directly upon the houses. With heavy kicks they smashed in the doors and rushed upon the occupants within. They soon put an end to these snipers.

But now, around one side of the town appeared a troop of Austrian horse.

Hal raised a cry of warning, and quickly the Cossacks turned and leaped upon their own horses; but the Austrian cavalry had no mind to give battle to their foes, and after pouring in a volley, turned and fled down the narrow mountain pass.

"After them!" cried Alexis.

He put spurs to his horse and dashed ahead, his men following closely.

The Austrians had not gone far when their leader called a halt and consulted with his subordinate officer. They were, the leader knew, not far from a point where he could expect reënforcements.

A plan was quickly formed. The Austrians divided into two parts. The foremost blocked the road–down which the Cossacks were rapidly approaching–near a turn, so as to remain unseen by the approaching enemy until almost the moment of contact. The second force stayed some rods behind the first, forming in two lines, one along each side of the road. Some were armed with lances and sabers, but many also carried rifles.

As for the Cossacks, all carried lances and revolvers.

The Russians went forward at a gallop. Alexis was expecting to overtake the enemy, but he was hardly prepared for the suddenness of the encounter.

Ere he could give an order, there came one loud, flaming, whistling discharge from that living barrier drawn up across the road. Alexis' horse reared, as did others of the troop. Some of the men came to a quick stop, others were borne forward by the impetus of their former speed, but reined in for orders. No man fell, though one groaned and two hurled epithets at the foe.

Alexis, now that he had his horse under control, drew his sword with his right hand, his pistol with his left, which also held the rein, and ordered his men to charge, to fire at the moment of contact, then to cut, slash and club.

The first line of Austrians, as soon as they had fired, retreated between the two lines of supports, stopping at some further distance to reform. The second line, being thus cleared of the first, poured a hail of bullets into the Cossacks as the latter were caught between them.

Many fell, but the others turned on the second barrier with furious force, some, however, rushing upon the reforming first line.

They were the best riders in the world, and many a one of them held his lance aloft in one hand, his revolver raised in the other, the rein loose on his horse's neck.

The Austrians and Alexis' foremost men fired at the same moment. The Austrians had not time to turn and flee, for the Cossacks, unchecked by this second greeting of fire, came on at headlong speed.

"At 'em, boys!" cried Hal excitedly, firing his revolver at a tall Austrian officer, who fell sidewise from his horse.

An Austrian officer struck with a sword at Chester's left arm, but only knocked the pistol from his hand. The lad found himself threatened on the right by a trooper, and slashed at him with his sword. The blow went home, but the sword's end became entangled with the victim's breast knot. A second trooper brought his rifle butt down heavily upon the sword, and it snapped off.

Chester felt a keen smart in his left leg. It came from a second sword blow aimed by the Austrian officer, who might have followed it with a third, but that he was now attacked elsewhere. Chester had no sooner clapped his hand to his wounded leg than he was stunned by a blow from the rifle butt of the trooper who had previously struck the sword. He fell forward on his horse's neck, which he grasped madly with both arms.

Still holding the broken sword in his right hand, Chester now lapsed from a sense of the tumult, the plunging and shrieking horses, the whir and clash of swords, the thuds of rifle blows, into half consciousness, while the unguided horse turned suddenly and made off in the direction from which he had come.

Meanwhile the Cossacks had been pushing the Austrians back. Hal and Alexis, fighting side by side, were so far unharmed. Right into the midst of the enemy they plunged, and for several minutes could see nothing but flying swords and lances. Then, at a signal, the Austrians turned and fled.

Hal turned to speak to Chester, but the latter was not there. In alarm, he called Alexis' attention to the fact that Chester was missing. Quickly Alexis ordered a halt and looked around. Bodies strewed the road, and leaping from their horses, the two investigated. Chester was not there.

"Great Scott!" exclaimed Hal. "What can have happened to him?"

Alexis questioned his men. One remembered that a great black charger had dashed through the troop in the midst of the battle and had fled to the rear. He remembered that a form was upon the animal's back.

"It must have been Chester," said Hal to Alexis. "Do you go on in pursuit of the Austrians, and I will go back and see if I can find him."

"Good," said Alexis. "The horse probably will run back to the main column. You should not have much trouble finding him."

With a word of command Alexis ordered the troop ahead, and Hal started back on the trail of his chum.

When Chester was again aware of things he was still clasping the horse's neck and was being borne along he knew not whither. His head ached and his left leg pained him greatly. He was dizzy and too weak to raise himself from his position. He could not hear any sound of fighting. He tried to sit up and look around, but this added to his pain, so he fell forward on the neck of his horse again.

Suddenly the horse stopped.

Once more Chester tried to sit up. This time he was successful, and in spite of the pain glanced about him. The horse had halted near a little house, set back some fifty feet from the road, and even as he looked up a woman came from the doorway. She started in astonishment at the sight of the horse and its wounded rider, and hastened back into the house. She reappeared in a moment, however, accompanied by a second woman, the latter armed with a huge revolver.

The two now approached the lad and lifted him from the horse. They supported him as he dragged himself into the house, and dropped weakly into a chair. Then the women stepped back and pointed the revolver at him.

"You shall remain here," she said, "until I can turn you over to the Austrians."

Chester was somewhat surprised. By the assistance given him by the women, he had thought that, after resting up, he would be allowed to rejoin his friends; but the set expression on the woman's face told the lad that she meant what she said.

The second woman approached with water and bandages and soon bound up his wounds. Then the lad was escorted to another room, which looked out upon the road. The woman mounted guard over him with her revolver.

"Some of our troops will be here before long," she told him. "Until then I shall guard you."

All this time Chester retained his hold on the broken sword. Suddenly, down the road, came the sound of a galloping horse. Chester glanced through the window and in a moment he had made out the figure of Hal. Quickly he stepped to the window, and before his captor could prevent him, shattered the window pane with his broken sword.

"Hal!" he cried at the top of his voice. "Hal! Here I am, wounded and a prisoner!"

The woman hurled herself upon the lad and bore him back out of sight. In his weakened condition he was no match for her. She thrust him back into the chair. He turned his eyes to the window. Hal had passed on.

"Great Scott!" ejaculated Chester. "He didn't hear me!"

But Hal had heard. He recognized the sound of his friend's voice, and realized that he was in trouble of some kind. Likewise he surmised what the trouble was, for he knew that they were in the heart of a hostile country. Therefore, he did not check the speed of his horse at once, but rode some distance further before drawing rein. Then he dismounted and tied his horse to a sapling.

Springing in among the trees, he advanced cautiously toward the house. Both women, secure in the belief that he had passed on, turned to taunt Chester. The latter shut his lips grimly and refused to make a reply.

Suddenly, from the next room, came a tremendous clattering of pots and pans.

Both women jumped to their feet.

"There is someone out there!" cried one of the women excitedly.

With her revolver pointed straight before her she moved softly toward the door. At the same moment Chester realized Hal's ruse and cried:

"Look out, Hal!"

128

CHAPTER XXII

AT BAY IN THE PASS

When Hal, after creeping into the house through a window, had inadvertently bumped into several pots and pans, knocking them to the floor with a clatter, he drew his revolver and stood stockstill. He heard Chester's cry of warning, and, realizing that an enemy was approaching, he drew a bead upon the doorway.

An arm with a pistol appeared through the opening; there was a flash of fire and a bullet sped past him. He fired quickly in return, and the weapon of his unseen enemy dropped to the floor with a crash, followed by a shrill scream of pain.

"Great Scott, a woman!" cried Hal and leaped forward.

But the woman was more frightened than hurt. Realizing that she was uninjured, as Hal came toward her, she leaped forward and threw her arms about him, pinioning the lad's hand that held his revolver to his side. At the same moment she cried out to her companion:

"Quick! Pick up the revolver and shoot him while I hold him!"

Hal realized that he was in grave danger and struggled fiercely to free his hands. But his adversary was a very powerful woman, and having gained a secure hold, Hal was unable to free himself.

The woman who had been left to guard Chester, at the command of the other, ran to her aid. Chester, holding to the back of the chair, drew himself to his feet and staggered after her, still clinging to his broken sword.

As the woman stooped to pick up the revolver dropped by the other when Hal's bullet had struck her hand, Chester, in spite of the pain of his wounds, leaped forward. As she arose to her feet and would have fired point-blank at Hal, he knocked the weapon from her hand with a sharp blow of his broken sword.

Then coming quickly to Hal's side he took the lad's revolver from him, and, stepping back, aimed it at the head of the woman with whom his friend was struggling.

"Release him instantly," he ordered, "or I shall fire!"

The woman glanced at him over her shoulder, and smiled tauntingly.

"You wouldn't shoot a woman," she sneered.

"I wouldn't like to," replied Chester, "but if you have not released him and if both of you do not line up against that wall with your hands in the air by the time I count three, I will shoot, just as surely as I stand here. One, two—"

The woman glanced at him. Her eyes must have told her that the lad meant what he said, for, releasing Hal, she stepped quickly back and raised her hands in the air. The second woman followed her example. Chester stepped to Hal's side, and extended the revolver to him.

"Take this quick!" he commanded.

Hal did so, and without another word, Chester suddenly crumpled up in a heap on the floor. He had fainted.

Still covering the women with his revolver, Hal knelt by his friend's side. Then he turned to the woman.

"Some water!" he commanded.

Under the threatening muzzle of the revolver, the woman brought it, and at a command from Hal, bathed Chester's face. Then, still at Hal's command, she lifted the lad and placed him in a chair. Hal took his seat near the window, for he knew that it was only a question of time until some of the Russian troops passed in one way or the other. His revolver still covered the two women, who sat without uttering a word.

Gradually the color returned to Chester's face, and at last he opened his eyes and looked about. He took in the situation at a glance, and smiled faintly.

"Well, I see we won," he said.

"We did," replied Hal grimly. "How do you feel?"

"Better. I shall be all right now."

"Do you think you are equal to holding this revolver while I go out and reconnoiter?"

"Sure!" replied Chester. "Give it to me."

Hal put the revolver in his friend's hand.

"Don't hesitate to fire if one of them makes a false move," he said. "They would kill you in a moment if they had the chance."

"I'll use it if necessary; have no fear about that," replied Chester.

Hal arose and left the room and the house. He gazed up and down the road. There was no sign of troops, nor, by listening intently, could he hear hoof beats. He made his way to where he had left his horse, and tied it alongside the horse that had brought Chester to the house. Then he returned to Chester and his prisoners.

"There is no telling how long we may have to wait for our men to return," he said to his friend. "Do you suppose that if I lifted you up on your horse you could ride?"

"I am sure of it," replied Chester.

"That is the best plan," said Hal. "Come, then, we will try it."

He went to Chester's side, and still holding the revolver in his right hand, threw his left arm around his friend's neck. Chester put an arm about Hal's shoulder, and thus supported, made his way from the room without much pain.

Hal made a stirrup of his hand, and Chester, putting his foot into it, was soon astride his horse, though he winced somewhat with the pain the exertion gave him. Then Hal sprang into his own saddle, and the two turned their horses' heads in the direction of the main body of Cossacks.

Along the narrow mountain trail they rode slowly for perhaps an hour without the sight of either friend or foe. Then, rounding a sharp turning in the pass, at the top of a steep section of the road, Hal reined in suddenly with a muttered imprecation. Chester followed his friend's example.

Perhaps half a mile away came a body of horsemen, perhaps twenty of them. The sun, shining upon their uniforms, showed them to be Austrians. Quickly Hal leaped from his horse, and putting forth his utmost strength, rolled several great stones into place across the road, absolutely barring the pass. Then, after Chester had been helped to the ground, the two lads dropped behind this barrier.

The pass at this point was hardly wide enough for four men to walk abreast. On each side walls of rock rose straight up for perhaps twenty feet. Hal looked at his two revolvers and the one he had taken from the women in the house.

"Lucky we have plenty of ammunition," he said calmly.

He tested all weapons carefully and loaded them. Then he passed one to Chester.

"I am keeping two," he explained, "because, being wounded, you probably won't be able to move about as quickly as I will. I don't know how long we shall be able to hold these fellows off; but if they don't rush us, we may be able to hold out till help arrives."

"If they were Germans I wouldn't feel quite so easy," said Chester; "but I don't believe there is much likelihood of Austrians rushing us."

"Right you are," said Hal cheerfully. "They'll probably dismount, hide behind their horses and try to pick us off."

As yet the Austrians were unaware of the presence of enemies in the pass above them. They came on slowly, laughing and talking. Then one, chancing to raise his head, saw the barrier in the pass. He called the attention of the others to it. No sign of an enemy was visible, but the Austrians approached very carefully.

The two lads waited until the Austrians were so close that a miss was impossible, then, taking deliberate aim, each fired once. Two of the enemy fell to the roadside.

There came a cry of dismay from the Austrians, and they reined in their horses and sprang to the ground.

But two of them had not been quick enough, and while they left their horses at practically the same time as did the others, they did not rise again to their feet.

"Four!" said Chester calmly.

"About ten, if Alexis were doing the counting," said Hal grimly. "But I would give a whole lot if he were here right now."

The Austrians forced their horses to lie down, and took up their positions behind them. Then they blazed away wildly at the barrier ahead. They could see nothing at which to shoot, however, and their bullets did no damage.

"I wonder if the Austrians know this old hat trick?" said Chester.

Picking up a little stick, he put his cap upon it and raised it slowly over the barrier. A hail of bullets flew about it. Chester took deliberate aim at one of the Austrians who exposed himself, and Hal at another. Again their revolvers cracked once each, and two Austrians bit the dust.

"We'll be on even terms soon, if we keep this up," said Hal gleefully.

Chester tried the cap trick again; but this time it did not work. The Austrians had learned a lesson.

For perhaps five minutes there was silence; then Hal, glancing quickly over the barrier, saw one of the enemy jump to his feet and dash straight toward the barrier. In his anxiety to pick the man off, Hal fired too quickly, and missed.

The man dashed on and flung himself to the ground right up against the barrier. Here, for the moment, he was safe, for the lads could not get at him without leaning over the barrier and thus exposing themselves to the fire of the others.

A second Austrian leaped to his feet and dashed forward. This time, however, Hal did not hurry, and picked the man off with ease. Hardly had his weapon spoken, when a shot from below went whizzing by his head. Hal tumbled back to safety rapidly.

"Great Scott!" he exclaimed. "We'll have to get that fellow away from there. He almost got me that time."

"Yes; but how?" demanded Chester.

Hal considered the situation for some moments in silence. Then he passed one of his two revolvers to Chester.

"You blaze away as rapidly as you can at the Austrians with those two guns," he said. "Never mind whether you see anything to shoot at or not. Just shoot when I give the word. That'll keep those fellows under cover. I'll attend to this one."

133

"What are you going to do?" asked Chester.

"I'm going over after him!" said Hal grimly.

"But he is liable to kill you!" exclaimed Chester in alarm.

"If I don't get him," said Hal quietly, "he is sure to kill us both before long. Here goes!"

At the moment that he sprang to the top of the barrier, Chester opened upon the Austrians with both weapons. The man on the opposite side of the barrier was taken by surprise by Hal's sudden action. Hal toppled over upon him without warning. With a startled cry the Austrian raised his weapon to fire, but Hal was too quick for him.

His revolver, less than a foot from the man's head, spoke sharply. Hal waited long enough to see that the work had been well done, then rose to his feet, placed his hand upon the barrier, and, amid a hail of bullets from the other Austrians, vaulted back to safety.

"I got him!" he told Chester quietly, as he turned and emptied his own revolver at the enemy, who seemed on the point of rushing forward.

Quickly Chester reloaded his own revolvers, and it was well that he did so, for the enemy seemed to be manifesting a desire to come forward to the attack, apparently believing that the lads were out of ammunition.

The lads had now accounted for eight of the enemy, but they were not so foolish as to believe that the Austrians would remain in their present position and be picked off one at a time.

"They'll make a rush soon!" declared Chester.

"Well," replied Hal, "when they do we'll be ready for 'em. We can shoot straighter than they can while they are on the run. We should be able to pick off two more each before they get here."

"We'll have a try at it," said Chester simply.

It was plainly evident that the Austrians were preparing for a move of some kind. Suddenly, at a given signal, all twelve of the foe still alive, sprang to their feet and made a concerted rush toward the barrier.

"Here they come!" cried Hal. "Steady now!"

CHAPTER XXIII

IN THE NICK OF TIME

Hal, at the right of the barrier, confined his attention to that side of the road, leaving Chester to deal with the enemy rushing forward on the left. Three times the weapon of each lad spoke, and at each shot an Austrian fell to the ground. Firing coolly and deliberately at such close quarters, a miss was absolutely impossible.

But the lads did not have time to fire again. The enemy was at the barrier; but, instead of hurling themselves over it, as both lads had expected they would, they dropped to the ground on the opposite side of the big rocks, and there they remained.

It was indeed a peculiar situation–the enemies less than six feet apart, separated only by a few rocks. Still the Austrians, in spite of their losses, outnumbered the lads three to one.

Now the rocks of the barrier began to move inward toward the lads.

"Great Scott!" cried Chester. "They are trying to push these rocks over on us. If they tumble this barrier over, we can't hope to account for all six of them."

The lads braced themselves against the rocks; but the strength of the two was not as great as the strength of the six. Such a contest could have but one ending. The boys realized this as well as did their foes.

"Well," said Hal calmly, "it looks as though they had us. All ready for a last stand, Chester?"

"All ready," replied Chester calmly.

"When I say jump," instructed Hal, "leap backward!"

Chester nodded in understanding of this plan.

"Now!" cried Hal. "Jump!"

Both lads leaped quickly backward, and as they did so, the barrier–freed of their supporting shoulders–tumbled inward, while the six Austrians sprawled on the ground. For a moment the lads had the advantage and they made the best of it.

Hal's revolver spoke and one Austrian straightened out in the act of rising. Chester accounted for another, and then both lads sprang in close upon the foe, thus precluding the use of the foe's firearms.

Hal, grappling with two of the enemy, was giving a good account of himself; but Chester, weak from the loss of blood, was unable to hold his own. A blow from the butt of one of the Austrian's revolvers and he went to the ground.

At that moment, from their rear, came the sound of rapidly galloping hoofs. Around the bend some distance away dashed a troop of Cossacks, Alexis himself at their head. The giant Cossack took in the situation with one comprehensive glance and put spurs to his horse. The two Austrians who had attacked Chester saw the advancing Cossacks, and, turning, took to their heels.

The two with whom Hal struggled, however, were too busily occupied to notice the approach of reënforcements and sorely, each trying to bring his revolver to bear.

Alexis now jumped from his horse and dashed forward toward the three. He stretched forth two mighty hands and plucked the Austrians off the lad. Raising each high in the air, he stretched wide his arms, and then brought them together with great force. There was a crunch as the heads of the two met with terrific force. Then they hung limp in the giant's hands. He hurled them from him with a disdainful gesture, and, snatching his revolver from its holster, dropped to his knee and fired two shots in quick succession at the two remaining enemy, who were fleeing down the road.

His aim was true, and as the last of the Austrians bit the dust, Alexis turned to where Chester lay and picked him up gently in his arms. From his canteen he poured water over the lad's face and soon came signs of returning consciousness. Then he laid him gently on the ground and turned to Hal.

He gazed first at the lad, then at the dead bodies of the enemy and then back to Hal.

"Hm-m-m," he said gruffly. "Quite a fight. But where would you have been if Alexis had not arrived so opportunely?"

"Dead, I guess," replied Hal quietly. "We owe you our lives, but there is no need to tell you that we are grateful."

"Not a bit," said Alexis. "Thanks from one brave man to another are never necessary; but did you see how easily I disposed of those four Austrians?"

"It was very pretty," replied Hal.

"Wasn't it?" cried the giant gleefully. "Still, it was a trifle. I remember the time that I—"

Hal walked over to Chester's side and bent down and so did not hear the story of Alexis' might. The giant looked sorrowfully after him for a moment, muttered to himself and then he walked after him.

Chester now sat up and looked about. His eyes rested on the dead bodies.

"Looks like Alexis had been here," he muttered, for he had not yet seen the giant.

Alexis heard him and his face glowed with pleasure.

"He is here," he said, stepping forward.

Chester's face lighted up.

"By Jove!" he exclaimed. "It is good to see you. We have wished several times in the last hour that you were with us. We needed you badly. However, you arrived just in time."

Alexis blushed like a schoolboy, for he was not used to hearing others praise his prowess.

"Yes, I did arrive in the nick of time," he said awkwardly. "But come, we must get away from here."

"Have you learned the strength of the enemy in the mountains?" asked Hal a few minutes later, as they rode along down the pass.

"I learned enough to make sure that, without infantry and artillery support, the cavalry will probably be annihilated," replied Alexis briefly. "By a dash, we might be able to reach the plains of Hungary, but without support we should end our days there. I shall counsel retreat."

"But I thought you would never counsel retreat?" said Hal, smiling.

"For myself, never!" replied the giant. "But there are more lives than mine depending upon this. Therefore I say retreat."

Alexis was as good as his word. Upon their return to the main column, Alexis was called into consultation with the commanding officer. He recounted what he had learned, and urged that the retreat be begun at once.

"There are half a million men in these hills," he informed his commander, "and they are trying to draw us on. We will be allowed to go so far, and then they will close in on us. One hundred or two hundred thousand, I don't mind. We could whip them with ease; but half a million are too many for sixty thousand. If we had not outdistanced our infantry and artillery, we might do it, but without them, no."

"Still," said the commanding officer, "I have set my heart on striking one more blow at the enemy. Would you counsel against it?"

"I am always in favor of striking one more blow at the enemy," replied Alexis. "I suppose I should counsel against it, but I will not."

"Good!" exclaimed his commander. "One decisive blow to the enemy in the hills, and then we shall fall back into Galicia. Now, where are the Austrians massed?"

"It will be extremely hazardous," said Alexis slowly, "but I guess it can be done. Fifteen miles straight along this mountain pass you come to a small plateau. I advanced that far myself. Encamped there are in the neighborhood of one hundred thousand of the enemy. By a quick and silent dash and a night attack, we may be able to deal them a crushing blow; but even so, we must fall back immediately. Even then we shall be greatly harassed by the foe."

"Well," said the commander, "we shall make the attack, come what may afterward."

Alexis saluted his commander and returned to where he had left the two lads, where he repeated his interview. Then he turned to Chester.

"It is too bad," he said, "that you will be unable to take part in the battle."

"But I shall take part in it," exclaimed the lad. "You don't think I am going to sit idle while there is fighting going on, do you?"

138

"I am afraid you cannot help yourself," replied Hal. "You will go with the advance, of course; but you will be kept well in the rear."

In vain did Chester protest. His commanding officer overruled all of his complaints, and at last the lad was forced to make his way to the rear of the Russian army. All that day the army rested, and it was not until the following afternoon that the signal was given for the advance, for the Russian commander had so timed his movement that he would come upon the enemy after nightfall.

It was indeed an imposing sight, these 60,000 men, able to march scarcely six abreast through the narrow mountain pass, moving hurriedly through the midst of the wild Carpathians. For miles they stretched out, but they advanced rapidly, and long before night the advance guard was within sight of the Austrian position.

This was made known to the Russian commander by his scouts; and still out of sight, the Cossacks halted.

The pass was considerably wider here, and the men spread out somewhat. Outposts were thrown out to guard against a counter surprise attack, and the men allowed to lie down and rest.

The battle formation was preserved, however, and the men fell to sleep upon their arms, each and every one ready to spring up and dash forward at a moment's notice.

And still the Austrians were unaware of their approach.

CHAPTER XXIV

THE SURPRISE

Stealthily the vanguard of the Cossacks crept forward afoot. They had dismounted that they might approach the enemy with less danger of being heard. Naked blades were held firmly in their hands; revolvers and hand grenades were ready. The night attack of the Cossacks was under way.

Not a shot had been fired. Silently they stole on toward the sleeping Austrian camp. Feeling perfectly secure in the mountain fastness and believing their position practically impregnable, the Austrians failed to keep vigilant watch.

Now the first line of Cossacks, at a whispered word of command, fell to the ground on their faces. A sentry walked directly toward them, but in the blackness of the night he did not make out the silent forms.

As he turned his back on them, one shadowy form rose quickly to his feet and moved swiftly forward. There was the sound of a brief struggle, a cry stifled in his throat and the Cossacks moved forward again.

A second and then a third time this operation was repeated. Three Austrian sentinels lay dead upon the ground; still the camp slept on, unsuspecting.

More swiftly now, other troops issued from the mountain pass and spread out in a great semi-circle over the plateau. For two hours this movement continued in the darkness. The first line of Cossacks stood ready to fire at the first sign of discovery, but, undiscovered, waited for the rest of the force to get in position.

A dog in the Austrian camp barked. Others took up the cry. A sentry, aware of some strange sensation, fired his rifle in the air. At the moment the last of the Cossacks issued from the mountain pass. These last troops were mounted and stood with bared lances awaiting the word to charge.

The huge Austrian camp stirred along its length, but at that instant the Cossacks sprang to action. Came quick commands from the officers, and the first line moved upon the Austrian camp at a dead run. A hail of revolver bullets sped through the canvas of the tents, striking down those who were yet asleep and reaping a toll of death among those who were dashing to arms. Then the Cossacks charged with cold steel.

In little parties, without the semblance of formation or discipline, the Austrians dashed from their tents to beat back this sudden attack. There was no time for them to fall into position. The Cossacks were upon them. Right into the heart of the enemy's camp rushed the fearless horde in a terrible charge, cutting, slashing, hewing their way through.

The Austrians, caught unprepared, gave ground. The Cossacks followed up their first advantage closely, pressing the enemy so that they had no time to get into battle formation. A squad of Cossacks sprang toward a battery of field pieces, quickly wheeled it into position, and opened fire on the fleeing Austrians. The execution was fearful. Men went down in heaps, and those that survived fled faster than before.

The surprise was complete. A terrible confusion reigned among the enemy. The Russians pursued them relentlessly. Here and there men threw down their arms and surrendered by the hundreds.

Other mountain batteries now had been seized by the Cossacks and turned upon the foe. For a mile the Cossacks pursued the beaten enemy; then drew off as suddenly as they had come. Prisoners were abandoned. Quickly the big guns were put out of commission, and the advance guard–now the rearguard–fell back slowly, protecting the retreat of those in front.

In almost less time than it takes to tell it, the Cossacks were again in the saddle and dashing back down the mountain pass.

The Austrians, for a moment, were unable to form in solid ranks. But, at length, under the command of their officers, they formed and gave chase. But the Cossacks had too great a start. The losses of the Austrians had been terrible, those of the Cossacks comparatively slight. In spite of the fact that they had been in the midst of the fighting, Hal and Alexis had escaped without injury.

Now the Austrian cavalry, having had time to form, scattered on each side of the pass and rode after the Cossacks. They came up with the rear guard, and from the sides poured in bullets, until they were forced to draw rein because of the treacherous nature of the ground on either hand. It was here that the Cossacks sustained their heaviest losses.

But the raid had been a success; there could be no doubt about that.

The Russian commander was elated as, in the midst of his men, he ordered the retreat; but as the retreat continued, it became more hazardous. Even as

Alexis had predicted, the mountains swarmed with the enemy, who rained bullets upon the Russian columns from every hand.

In spite of this, however, by noon of the following day the Cossacks had reached the spot from which they had started the day before; and here a halt was called. Videttes were placed and the troops settled down for a brief rest. While they made a good mark for the guerillas, they nevertheless were in too great force to permit of an attack in force.

Night fell, and once more the troops sprang to the saddle and continued their retreat. Morning found the vanguard well out of the mountains on the plains of Galicia, and soon the last of the rear guard had issued from the pass. Then the mighty columns spread out. There was no pursuit, and the commander ordered the retreat conducted more slowly.

Two days later the columns of raiding Cossacks rode in among the Russian troop besieging the Galician city of Cracow. Here the commander decided to remain until he should receive instructions from the Grand Duke. He dispatched Chester, who had now recovered sufficiently from his wounds as to be feeling perfectly fit, Hal and Alexis to carry word of the expedition to the Grand Duke. So the three friends again set out upon a journey.

They traveled without haste and without incident and at length found themselves once more in Lodz. Here all three reported to the Russian commander-in-chief. After receiving his congratulations, and while they yet stood in his presence, there came a terrible roar from outside the tent.

The Grand Duke listened intently. Thousands upon thousands of voices rose on the air. They were cheering. Thousands upon thousands of voices took up the cry:

"God save the Czar!"

The Grand Duke advanced rapidly toward the entrance to his tent. The two lads and the giant Cossack made as if to depart; but the Grand Duke, with a movement of his hand, signified for them to stay and so they remained.

The sound of cheering drew nearer. The Grand Duke left the tent, and through the door the lads could see him standing with bared head. Came the sound of galloping hoofs, and a cavalry troop drew up at the Grand Duke's tent. The latter stepped forward, and giving his hand to a brilliantly uniformed man, assisted him to dismount. Then, bowing low, he escorted his visitor into his tent.

As they appeared in the small enclosure Alexis fell upon his knee, and bowed till his head all but touched the ground.

Nicholas, the Czar of all the Russias, turned toward the three with a question on his lips. But the Grand Duke spoke first:

"These, sire, are three of your majesty's bravest soldiers, who have only now returned from a successful raid into the heart of the Carpathians."

The Czar glanced at the two lads.

"But these," he said, pointing his finger at Hal and Chester, "are not Russians."

"No, sire," replied the Grand Duke. "They are American lads; but they have rendered invaluable services to our cause," and while the lads stood listening, he gave the Czar a brief account of some of their experiences.

The Czar advanced and placed a hand upon the shoulder of each.

"I am glad," he said in perfect English, "to know you; and I envy my cousin George the services of such gallant youths."

Both lads bowed in acknowledgment of this compliment, and the Czar turned to Alexis, who was still kneeling.

"And this man," he said, "surely he is one of my Cossacks?"

"Yes, your majesty," replied the Grand Duke. "There is not a braver in the whole army," and he related some of Alexis' feats, as told him days before by Hal and Chester.

The Czar stretched forth a hand to Alexis, and the latter kissed it.

"You shall be remembered," said the Russian monarch.

Alexis' face glowed with pleasure. He was so taken by surprise that he was unable to speak.

The Grand Duke now signified that the three might leave the tent, and they accordingly bowed themselves out. Outside Alexis could restrain himself no longer.

"I told you I was a brave man!" he cried; "but I am even braver than I thought. I have been addressed by the Czar!"

An officer entered the Grand Duke's tent, and departed a moment later in great haste. A second later and the shrill call of a bugle carried through the town. It was the order for inspection. The Czar was about to review his troops.

An hour later Czar Nicholas stood before his army, or such a part of it as could be crowded in the plain before the Grand Duke's tent. Far out it stretched on all sides. In a short address, in which he praised his troops for their gallantry in action, the Czar predicted that success would eventually crown the Russian arms. Then he turned to an officer of the Grand Duke's staff and gave a command.

Immediately the latter approached Hal, Chester and Alexis, who, being apart from their regiments, stood a little to one side watching the ceremonies.

"Follow me!" he commanded.

Without a word the three obeyed. Straight to the Czar the officer led the way, the two lads and the Cossack wondering what it was all about. In front of the Russian monarch the officer withdrew, leaving them alone before the Czar.

The Russian ruler stepped between the three, with a smile on his face drew something from his pocket, approached each in turn and pinned something on his breast.

Alexis, Hal and Chester let their eyes drop to these objects, and all three cried out in surprise.

For the Czar of Russia, there in the presence of the army of Poland, before the Grand Duke and other Russian nobles and dignitaries, with the eyes of the entire assemblage focused upon them, had pinned upon the breasts of the two American lads and the giant Cossack the Cross of the Order of St. George!

It was their reward for bravery, and a great cheer went up from the assembled hosts.

CHAPTER XXV

A NEW MISSION

The two lads were again having an audience of the Grand Duke. The latter, after ordering them to bear word to the commander of the Cossack force that had invaded the Carpathians to remain before Cracow until further notice, had also proposed a new mission to the lads.

"I would like to learn," he said, "whether there is any truth in the report that, in the event we capture Cracow, the population of Galicia will come to our support and throw off the Austrian yoke. Of course I have heard these rumors from apparently reliable sources, but I would prefer to know the truth from someone I can trust implicitly."

"We shall be glad to undertake that mission, Your Excellency," said Hal. "I believe that by using a little strategy we can gain entrance to the city. It would probably be easier for us than for one of your own men, because we are Americans and may be able to use that to advantage."

"I had thought of that," replied the Grand Duke. "In fact, it is for that reason that I selected you. I will give you a message to your commander, relieving you from active duty. My advice is that you do not take Alexis on this mission. He would probably hinder you."

The boys saluted, and taking the paper the Grand Duke extended to them, departed. On their way back toward Cracow they informed Alexis of their mission and of the fact that he was not to accompany them. The Cossack was disappointed and astonished.

"Not take me!" he exclaimed in surprise. "Why, I am good for fifty men! You know that!"

"But this is not a case of strength and fighting," Hal explained. "This is a case where strategy will count more than a hundred men."

"Well," demanded Alexis, "am I not a strategist? Did you not tell me so with your own lips? As a strategist there is none better than I. Why, I can tell you how I—"

"But, Alexis," Hal interrupted, "one look at you would tell an Austrian your nationality. You cannot expect to fool them as we did the peasant of the hills. I am sorry, but there is no help for it."

Alexis was greatly crestfallen, but he admitted the truth of the boys' reasoning.

"It is true that anyone would know I am a Cossack," he replied, "but if it came to a fight—"

"If it comes to a fight," said Chester, "we shall miss you greatly; but we shall have to try and get along without you this time."

Back with their regiment they gave the message releasing them from active duty to their commander; then, changing their uniforms for civilian garb and bidding Alexis good-by, they set out in the direction of the Galician stronghold, making a wide detour so as to approach from the north, rather than from the direction of the Russian troops in the East.

They went horseback, and they rode slowly, for they did not wish to attract undue attention to themselves by too great speed. The route they traversed made it a good two-days' journey, and long before coming to the city proper they encountered bands of Austrian troops. To these, however, they paid little heed and they were not molested.

"Evidently they don't care who goes in," remarked Chester.

"Looks that way," replied Hal; "but I'll bet they pay strict attention to anyone who tries to get out. That's where our hardest work probably will come in."

"I guess you are right," said Chester.

Nevertheless they were halted by an Austrian patrol when close to the city. To him, however, they explained that they were American tourists, caught in Galicia at the outbreak of the war, and that they had penetrated beyond the Austrian lines without being aware of it.

"We want to get back to safety," Hal told him.

The Austrian officer smiled and let them pass without further words. Inside the Galician city the lads prowled about leisurely. The extreme eastern end of the city was a mass of ruins. The shells hurled by the big Russian guns had done great damage; but the flames had been extinguished before they had reached the heart of the city, and as the Russians had later fallen back a considerable distance the city now was perfectly quiet.

Night came on, and the lads sought shelter in the home of a Galician peasant. The house was small but comfortable, and the old man who lived in it admitted them without question. They repeated to him the story told the Austrian officer, adding that the place in which they had been staying had been destroyed by a Russian shell.

"And your sympathies," inquired the old man, "are with the Austrians?"

"Of course," replied Hal quietly, "Russian barbarism must be wiped out."

"Good!" replied the old man. "I suppose you know there is considerable sentiment in favor of the Russians, however?"

"I have heard something to that effect; but I could scarcely credit it," replied Hal guardedly.

"Well," said the old man, "it is true. A plot was discovered not two days ago to give the city into the hands of the Russians. The conspirators were arrested right here in my house. They were friends of mine. I was known to be loyal, and my false friends took advantage of that fact to do their plotting here. Now my house is watched closely, although they have hesitated to arrest me."

The old man made the two comfortable for the night and left them. Before preparing for bed the lads talked over what the old man had told them. As they were getting ready to retire, they heard voices from an adjoining room.

Through a little hole in the wall they could see a stream of light. Hal put his eye to the hole. In the room beyond he made out the figures of two Austrian officers. Then the lad motioned to Chester to remain silent, and laid his ear to the hole.

"You are sure of this other plot?" came a voice.

"Perfectly; but we will nip it in the bud. There is no question but the people would welcome a Russian investment of the city. Galicia is practically in sympathy with the Russians. We have been hard put to it to keep them from rising and turning the city over to the Czar's troops."

"Well, I am sure we are equal to any occasion," said the first speaker.

Hal turned away from the wall and repeated the conversation to Chester.

"I guess that's all we need to know," he added.

"I should say it is," was the reply. "Now the question is, how are we to get back to our own lines?"

"I have a plan that may work," said Hal. "It came to me a moment ago."

"And that is?" prompted Chester.

"Well," said Hal quietly, "we will exchange clothes with those two officers in the next room."

"Good!" cried Chester.

"Let's start then."

"Hadn't we better wait until they are asleep?"

"No; I believe I have a better plan. Come with me."

Quietly the two lads slipped from the room and down the little hall. Then they turned and made their way back again, coming only as far as the door to the Austrians' room. Hal opened it and walked in. At sight of the two Austrian officers he drew back in well-simulated surprise.

"I beg your pardon," he exclaimed. "I am in the wrong room."

"Oh, that's all right," laughed one of the Austrians. "Are you the Americans who are stopping here?"

"Yes," replied Hal.

"Well," said the Austrian. "It's early yet; come in and have a chat with us. You can perhaps tell us some things about America that we would like to know."

Hal accepted the invitation, mentally congratulating himself upon their good fortune. After a lengthy conversation, Hal rose to go.

"It's getting late," he said. "Come, Chester, we may as well turn in."

Chester also rose. In going to the door it was necessary for Hal to pass behind one of the Austrians. As he did so, he quickly threw out a hand and clutched the man by the throat. At the same moment Chester sprang upon the second unsuspecting officer, and the cry that the latter would have let out was stifled in his throat by the pressure of the lad's fingers.

148

Hal now produced a revolver, and Chester did likewise. They covered the two officers.

"One outcry and you are dead men," said Hal calmly.

While Chester kept them covered, Hal bound and gagged them. Then the two lads stripped them of their uniforms, which they donned themselves. Feeling perfectly secure in these, the lads saw that the prisoners were well tied and unable to cry out, and then left the room, shutting the door behind them.

In the hall they encountered their host, but the latter, recognizing the Austrian uniform, did not even speak to them. The lads left the house quietly, and turned their faces toward the north, intending to go back by the way they had come.

Several times they were spoken to by Austrian officers as they walked along the streets, but to these salutations they made no reply, trusting that their apparent rudeness would cast no suspicion upon them. And it did not.

At length they came to the farthest Austrian outpost, and here, for the first time they were challenged. Hal stepped a little ahead of Chester and spoke.

"We are inspecting the lines," he said calmly.

"You cannot pass here," came the reply. "My orders are to shoot anyone who attempts to get by. The general himself couldn't pass. You will have to go back."

"Oh, all right, if that's the way you feel about it," said Hal, turning his back upon the sentry.

The sentry, believing that the lads would go away, lowered his rifle, and in that moment Hal turned quickly again and sprang upon him. A quick blow knocked the sentry from his feet, and the lads dashed forward. In the distance Hal made out the form of several horses, and the lads ran toward them.

"Quick, Chester!" cried Hal.

But the Austrian sentry had not been knocked unconscious. He was only stunned. He staggered to his feet, brought his rifle to his shoulder and fired. He was too unsteady to aim carefully, however, and the lads were unhurt.

But the sound of the shot aroused the Austrian camp. Men came rushing forward.

The boys leaped to the backs of two horses and spurred on.

"It's a race for life, Hal!" shouted Chester, as the horses dashed ahead.

CHAPTER XXVI

A DASH FOR LIFE

One glance over his shoulder convinced Hal that at least half a dozen of the enemy had mounted and were spurring forward in pursuit. He passed the word to Chester, and bending low in their saddles, the lads urged their horses to greater efforts.

From ahead suddenly came a body of horsemen. Before they realized it, the lads were dashing by these at a distance of less than a hundred yards. Here the Austrian uniforms stood them in good stead. The officer hesitated to give a command to his men to fire on what were apparently Austrian officers, and before he was made aware of the situation by shouts from behind, the lads had placed considerable distance between themselves and these new enemies.

Now the latter also turned and gave chase.

After some minutes the lads realized that they were easily maintaining their lead and breathed easier.

"We'll get away yet if our horses don't give out!" shouted Chester.

"All right!" Hal shouted back. "Keep up the pace!"

In their haste in seizing upon two horses, the lads had not had time to look the animals over and it soon developed that they had made a bad choice. The animals which the boys bestrode had returned only an hour before from a long and tedious journey, and consequently were almost exhausted. Under the spur they put forth their best efforts, but finally they began to tire, and despite the urging of the lads, faltered in their stride.

Hal was the first to notice this.

"I am afraid it is all up!" he shouted to Chester.

Right in the face of his oncoming enemies he drew rein. Chester followed his example, and then both lads quickly dismounted.

At this spot there was a small clump of trees. Slapping their horses across the flanks with their hats, the lads plunged in among the foliage while the tired horses made off slowly.

"Up into these trees quick," shouted Chester. "It has saved us before; it may again!"

Quickly the lads clambered up among the branches, where they lay perfectly still. The sound of the approaching Austrians grew nearer, and at last half a dozen of the enemy pulled up their mounts almost under the lads' hiding place.

"Which way did they go?" asked a voice.

"They have probably made off through the woods," said a second. "We'll have to search for them."

The tree in which the lads were hiding was the largest nearby. Up in its dense foliage the boys were absolutely hidden from the ground below. One of the Austrians glanced up into the tree.

"They may be hiding up here," he said to his companions.

"Hardly likely," replied a second.

"Well, I'll send up a couple of shots and see," said the first speaker.

His rifle spoke sharply twice. Hal felt a slight stinging sensation in his left arm. One of the bullets, as it passed, brushed his skin. The other sang close to Chester's head. But in spite of this, and in spite of the fact that another shot from below might end one of their lives, neither boy so much as shifted his position.

After firing the shot into the tree the Austrian became still, listening, as did his companions. There was no sound.

"They can't be up there," said a voice. "If they were, and even had not been hit, they couldn't remain still."

"You are right," said another voice. "We shall have to look for them elsewhere. Scatter out, men, and we'll search the woods."

The Austrians moved from beneath the tree. Waiting until he was sure that they had gone, Chester whispered to Hal:

"What shall we do now?"

"If possible," replied Hal, "we shall slip down and try to pick out a couple of fresh horses. Then we can make another dash for it."

"All right," agreed Chester, "but we had better wait here until we can get down the tree unseen."

Hal nodded in assent, and for perhaps half an hour the lads waited silently. In the distance they could hear the enemy beating up the bushes for some trace of them, but these sounds gradually grew farther away; then died down altogether.

Cautiously Hal peered down from his hiding place. There was no sign of an enemy. The lad dropped quickly to the ground, and Chester followed suit a moment later. Then they dashed silently toward the road.

Upon entering the woods in pursuit of the fugitives, the Austrians had abandoned their horses and were searching afoot. Approaching the edge of the forest, the lads saw six horses tied to trees. They ran rapidly toward them. As they did so a single Austrian, who had been left to guard the animals, stepped suddenly forward, raised his rifle and cried: "Halt!"

There was no time for either lad to draw his revolver. Chester's hand went to his pocket, even as he ran, but he did not wait to extract the weapon. With his hand still in his pocket, he pointed the muzzle of his revolver at the Austrian and pressed the trigger. The bullet sped true through the cloth, and the Austrian dropped his rifle and toppled over to the ground.

"Good work, Chester!" shouted Hal, not pausing in his stride toward the horses.

He had all six horses untied in a jiffy, and passing the bridle of one to his chum, leaped lightly into the saddle. Chester did likewise. The other horses stood still.

"No use leaving them here for the enemy to pursue us with," decided Chester.

He rode his own horse among the others, and with several quick blows of his cap, started them on ahead of them.

At that moment, the Austrians who had been scouring the woods for the fugitives, attracted by the sound of the shot, came into sight and dashed toward the lads, their revolvers spitting fire as they ran.

153

"Come on!" cried Hal to Chester.

It was no time to hesitate, nor to fight back while there was a chance of getting away. Putting spurs to their horses both lads were soon out of range.

"Now," said Chester, "we shall have to keep a sharp lookout for other Austrians in front; for it is certain all of our pursuers didn't enter the woods after us."

"Right you are," replied Hal.

They rode forward at a quick trot, and soon were out of sight of the enemy behind. For perhaps fifteen minutes they continued on their way without interruption, and then a band of horsemen bore down on them.

"Austrians," said Chester briefly. "What shall we do?"

"Go straight ahead," replied Hal quickly. "Perhaps they will not recognize us. We still have our Austrian uniforms. It may be they will take us for some of the searching party."

They drew nearer the approaching horsemen. The latter reined in their mounts.

"Did you find them?" Hal called out.

"No," came back the reply; "did you?"

"No," said Hal, "they must have given us the slip."

The horsemen came closer and Hal and Chester kept their faces averted as much as possible, for they knew that a close scrutiny would betray their identity.

"Well," shouted Hal, "we will look a little farther on. You search the woods. Perhaps your eyes may be better than ours."

"All right," was the reply, and the boys rode on slowly so as to give their mounts a rest. Some moments later there was a great commotion behind, and turning in their saddles, the lads saw the Austrians coming rapidly after them. They had come upon the little party who had seen the lads leaving the woods.

With a cry to Chester, Hal put spurs to his horse and soon both were literally flying over the ground, the Austrians in full chase.

But the horses that the boys now bestrode were much fresher than had been their first mounts; still, Hal saw that several of the Austrians were gaining.

Now one of the enemy drew well ahead of his companions, a bit behind came a second, while a third, who was some distance ahead of the remainder, closely followed the second. These three, at their respective distances, slowly drew closer to the lads.

Suddenly, without a word to Hal, Chester checked his horse abruptly, and his revolver flashed in his hand. Before the first Austrian could check his mount, he had come within range of the lad's weapon, which spoke sharply. The Austrian tumbled sidewise from his horse.

Chester turned and spurred on after Hal.

Now the second Austrian drew close upon the lad. Once more the latter abruptly checked his horse and turned to face the Austrian. The latter, perceiving the boy's maneuver, also drew rein. But he was not quick enough, and a second bullet from Chester's revolver laid him low. Once more the lad turned his horse's head forward and dashed on.

The third Austrian, unmindful of the fate that had overtaken his two companions, still dashed after the lads. He gained steadily, and was now a considerable distance ahead of the main body of the enemy. A third time Chester turned suddenly on the foe and a third time his revolver spoke. He missed, and the Austrian opened with his own revolver. But his aim was no better.

Chester, sitting quietly on his horse, then took careful and deliberate aim and at his next shot, the Austrian fell to the ground. Then he turned and rode on after Hal, who had slowed down to wait for him.

Once more the lads put spurs to their horses and dashed on–each forward stride of their animals taking them much nearer the Russian lines and safety–until at last they made out in the distance the outposts of the Russian camp.

Hal raised a cry of triumph, but at the same moment his horse stepped into a hole and went to his knees, hurling Hal over his head.

155

Chester reined in alongside his friend and leaped to the ground. The Austrians, perceiving the lad's misfortune, bore down on them with a wild cry of joy.

CHAPTER XXVII

SAFE

In spite of his tumble, Hal was uninjured and sprang quickly to his feet. Chester turned to the prostrate horse, and attempted to get it to its feet. The horse moaned with pain, and Chester gave up the attempt, for he realized in an instant that the animal had broken its leg in the fall.

With revolvers in hands, both lads turned to face their foes.

"We won't give up without a fight!" declared Hal grimly.

"No, we won't give up without a fight!" Chester agreed.

Standing behind the horse that was still on its feet the two lads pointed their weapons at the foe, who bore down upon them at top speed. There were at least a score of them, and the boys realized that the encounter could have but one end. Still they were determined to fight it out.

But now, from the rear, came a fierce yell. Turning their eyes momentarily in that direction, the lads beheld a welcome sight. Mounted on their superb chargers and galloping forward as swiftly as the wind, came a full squadron of Russian Cossacks; and as they came on, with loose-hanging reins, waving their weapons in the air, the fierce Cossack yell split the air time after time.

The Austrians hesitated; then, not mindful to retreat and allow their victims, whom they had followed so far, to escape scot-free they advanced on the lads again. Chester calmly picked off the first man on the right, and Hal disposed of the first man on the left. Realizing that assistance was on the way, the boys fought coolly and with determination, keeping the rearing and plunging horse always between them and their foes.

But this protection was soon removed. An Austrian bullet struck the horse in the head and he fell to the ground. Quickly the lads dropped behind the prostrate body and continued to pop away at their enemies. Two more went down, and still the lads were uninjured. The Cossacks were still some distance away, although approaching with the swiftness of the wind. The Austrians, seeking to end the encounter, spread out, fan-wise, and drew in upon the lads from three sides. The lads shifted their positions so as still to face all their foes. Then the Austrians came forward on a charge.

But they had delayed too long, for now the onrushing Cossacks had come within range, and a powerful voice rang out:

"Faster!"

In response to this command, the gallant chargers of the Cossacks leaped forward. A volley rang out, and bullets whistling over the heads of Hal and Chester found lodgment in Austrian breasts and heads. The enemy turned and fled.

With a quick word of command to his men the Cossack captain, now close to the kneeling lads, pulled in his horse with a sudden movement and sprang to the ground. The rest of the troop continued its mad dash after the Austrians, who were fleeing as fast as their tired horses could carry them.

There was but one possible result of such a chase. Noble animals, though the Austrian horses were, they were no match, at their best, for the Cossack chargers. And there was no mercy in the hearts of the Cossacks for their enemies. The Austrians did not cry for quarter, and no quarter was given. Ten minutes later the Cossacks, their ranks thinned by four, returned to where their leader had dismounted beside the lads.

As the Cossack commander flung himself to the ground by their side, both lads gave a cry of glad surprise.

"Alexis!" they exclaimed in a single voice.

"The same!" replied their Cossack friend. "Don't tell me any more about your strategy. Where would you have been, if I hadn't arrived just now, eh?"

"Well," said Chester slowly, "we wouldn't be here."

"You would have been dead, that's where you would have been," said Alexis calmly. "As it was, I almost arrived too late. Perhaps next time you will not leave me behind."

"We won't try to thank you," said Hal. "But how did you happen to arrive so opportunely?"

"Why," replied Alexis, "looking across the plain I saw two horsemen pursued by many others. I knew you would return from that direction, and I surmised who it was. But here is one case where my keen eyesight almost worked to your disadvantage. I made out your Austrian uniforms, even as I would have ordered my men forward, and hesitated. It wasn't any of my business if two Austrians were killed. Then I remembered your talk of strategy, and guessed that maybe the uniforms were part of it. But, you may take my word for it, you almost used too much strategy."

Alexis now ordered one of his men to secure two of the riderless horses, and, mounting, the lads rode back toward the Russian lines with the Cossack troop. Here they wasted no time, but started at once on their return journey to Lodz, Alexis, having obtained permission from his superior officer, going with them.

Grand Duke Nicholas was well pleased with the lads' report and complimented them highly upon their bravery and resourcefulness. Then he added, somewhat sorrowfully, the lads thought:

"I shall indeed be sorry to lose you."

"To lose us!" exclaimed Chester, in surprise. "Why, Your Excellency, we have no intention of being killed."

"I didn't mean that," replied the Grand Duke, with a slight smile, "but I have other work of importance for you. In fact, I may say of greater importance than any which you have yet accomplished."

"And we shall be glad to undertake it, no matter what it is," said Hal. "I am sure we can carry it through successfully."

"So am I," replied the Grand Duke dryly. "After some of the things you have done, I would not say there is anything you cannot do."

"But this new mission?" questioned Hal.

"The new mission," replied the Grand Duke, "will carry you back into France."

"What!" exclaimed both lads in surprise.

"Exactly," said the Grand Duke. "That is why I said I would be sorry to lose you, for I know that, once back with the British troops, you will not return again to Russia."

"Well, Your Excellency," said Chester, "we have seen service with the Cossacks, and we like it immensely, but—"

"But," interrupted the Grand Duke, "you would much prefer to be fighting with the English, your own people, or a kindred people, at least. Is that it?"

Both lads bowed in assent.

"It is, Your Excellency," replied Hal.

"Well," said the Grand Duke, "so be it."

He drew from his pocket a document, which he placed in Hal's hands.

"This," he said, "you will place in the hands of either Sir John French, the British commander, or General Joffre, the French commander-in-chief. I could, of course, send the message by wireless to London, but it would be intercepted by the Germans, and, while it naturally would be sent in code, I am not at all sure that the Germans could not decipher it."

"When shall we start, Your Excellency?" asked Chester.

"Whenever it is convenient," was the reply. "And the manner of your going I leave entirely to you. I will not hamper you with instructions."

"Your Excellency," said Hal, struck with a sudden thought.

"Yes?"

"I should like to make a request."

"Consider it granted," said the Grand Duke.

"Well, then," said Hal, "I should like to ask permission to take Alexis with us."

The Grand Duke was plainly surprised.

"He may be of great aid to us in getting through," Hal explained. "His strength is prodigious, and more than once, as I have told you, has stood us in good stead."

"Well," said the Grand Duke thoughtfully, "I will not order him to accompany you, for he would be out of his element on the other side; but, if he is willing to go, he has my permission."

After some further talk the boys took a friendly farewell of the commander-in-chief of the Russian armies and left the tent. They hunted up Alexis immediately.

"Well, Alexis," said Hal, "to-morrow we start back for France!"

The giant Cossack was on his feet in a moment.

"You mean you are going away for good?" he asked.

"Yes," replied Chester.

Alexis, although not an emotional man, was stirred deeply. The boys realized it in an instant; but he was not the man to give way to his feelings, and he said simply:

"I am sorry. I wish that you would remain here."

Then Hal broached his plan.

"Alexis," he said, "how would you like to come with us?"

The giant looked at him in surprise.

"Go with you?" he exclaimed. "To France?"

"Yes."

"But what would I do in France?" he questioned.

"Fight!" replied Chester briefly.

"True!" muttered Alexis.

"The Grand Duke has given his permission, if you desire to go," said Hal, "and we would indeed be glad to have you. We have grown very fond of you."

"And I of you," replied Alexis.

"In France," said Chester, "there are no such men as you. You would be a veritable Hercules, a man among men. Brave men there are there in plenty, but none such as you."

His vanity thus appealed to, Alexis saw the matter in a different light. He slapped one great fist down upon the table in a mighty blow.

"I'll go!" he shouted.

CHAPTER XXVIII

ON NEUTRAL SOIL

"Surely you are not afraid, Alexis?" exclaimed Chester.

"Afraid!" shouted Alexis. "Of course I am not afraid. But"–he eyed the large aëroplane dubiously–"but a man was not made to fly about in the air like a bird, particularly a man of my weight. Besides, I do not like great height. If I stand upon a precipice, I am immediately struck with the notion that I must jump off. If I jumped from an aëroplane I might upset it."

Both Hal and Chester laughed.

"I was that way myself once," said Chester, "so I know just how you feel. Many a man, otherwise very brave, has that same horror of height. However, you will soon get used to it."

"Maybe so," said Alexis dubiously. "However, if one man can fly, why, so can I. I am willing to take a chance."

"Good!" exclaimed Hal. "Now to get started."

Leaving Lodz, the three had made their way north, keeping as close to the German border as was safe, until they had reached Riga, on the Gulf of Riga, which extends in from the Baltic Sea. Here they had at first thought of going part of the distance by boat, but, because of the likelihood of the approach of German warships in the Baltic, had given up this plan and decided upon an aëroplane.

"We came to Russia in an airship," Hal had said. "We might as well go back in one. Besides, it is quicker."

And so it was agreed.

Ten miles south of Riga, surrounded by Russian airmen, they climbed into the craft which the Russian commander in the little city had provided for them. The plane was large and roomy, having a seating capacity of five.

Hal took his place at the steering wheel and Chester climbed aboard.

Still eyeing the flying craft suspiciously, Alexis followed Chester, and, sitting down suddenly, took hold of the seat with both hands and hung on for dear life, although the craft was still upon the ground. Then he lowered his head and shut his eyes.

Hal gave the word, and willing hands started the machine along the ground. Gradually it gained momentum until it was skimming over the ground at a rapid gait. Then Hal threw over the elevating lever, and the machine shot into the air amid the cheers of the Russians below.

Alexis was conscious of a sinking sensation in the region of his stomach, and he ducked his head even lower as the car rose higher in the air.

"Look up, Alexis!" shouted Chester, reaching over and laying a hand on the Cossack's arm.

Now that the machine had reached a good height, Hal held it steady, and it darted ahead on a straightaway course. The plane shook with the vibrations of the engine, but otherwise there was scarcely a noticeable motion.

Now that the machine was more steady, Alexis, in response to Chester's command, slowly opened his eyes and looked about. Seeing nothing, he closed them again immediately, and again ducked his head. Once more Chester yelled at him to look about, and at last Alexis raised his head and glanced into the distance.

"This is a terrible place for a man to be," he muttered with a shudder. "If man were meant to fly he would have been given wings. It is tempting the wrath of the elements to be here."

As he looked about him, however, and became conscious of the steadiness of the craft, his composure returned, and soon he was making inquiries regarding the construction of the craft, its speed and the height to which it could ascend. He glanced over the side of the machine, and then looked quickly upward again. The one glance below had made him ill.

He smiled faintly. "I can't look down yet," he said ruefully. "I suppose I'll get used to it in time; but now I had better keep my eyes inside."

"How fast are we going, Hal?" asked Chester.

"Sixty-five miles an hour," was Hal's reply.

Alexis was astonished.

"Sixty-five miles!" he ejaculated. "Why, it seems as if we were standing still."

"If we were close enough to the earth you would soon notice the difference," said Chester.

For another hour they continued on their way without incident, and then Chester discovered the dim outline of a second aircraft trailing them at a distance. It was not gaining, but even when Hal put on more speed, at a word from Chester, he was unable to shake it off.

"Evidently a German," said Chester. "I suppose he wants to see where we are going."

For another hour the plane pursued them. Then Chester perceived that there were two instead of one, and that both were creeping up on them.

With a cry to Hal, Chester picked two rifles from the bottom of the car.

"We'll have to fight them off!" he cried.

Alexis stirred uneasily in his seat.

"I was afraid of it," he muttered. "Now, what will happen to me when I go hurtling through space to the ground below?"

He shuddered.

Hal, in response to a command from Chester, slowed down suddenly. Taking careful aim at one of the pursuers, Chester emptied the magazine of his first rifle. There came from behind the sounds of screams, followed by an explosion.

"What was that?" cried Alexis in alarm.

"I got one of them!" replied Chester calmly. "The plane has gone to earth."

The second pursuing plane reduced its speed, but still clung on the trail of its would-be prey.

"We'll have to dispose of it some way, Hal," shouted Chester. "Turn quickly and run toward it, and I'll see if I can't send it to the ground."

He held his rifle ready as he spoke. Reducing the speed of the craft a trifle, Hal brought its head about in a wide circle; then darted suddenly toward the enemy.

But the latter was not caught unprepared, and a rifle bullet whistled close to Alexis' ear.

The giant Cossack clapped a hand to his head and for the first time looked toward the enemy. Then, reaching to the bottom of the machine, he raised up with a weapon, and, aiming at the hull of the enemy in the distance, poured the entire contents of the magazine into it. At the same moment a well-directed shot from Chester's rifle struck the pilot. He sprang to his feet, spun around crazily, and plunged from the car. A moment later and the aëroplane blew up with a loud bang.

Alexis, who had seen the pilot go overboard, let out a cry of dismay. He could not help but think of the terrible fall to the ground.

"Good work, Alexis!" cried Chester. "I told you you would get used to it before long."

"I am not used to it," replied the giant, "but when a bullet whistles past my ear I get mad. I just naturally have to fight back."

Nevertheless he made a brave effort to appear unconcerned, and he took a look over the side. At that moment Hal allowed the car to glide slowly nearer the earth. For a moment Alexis was unaware of this sinking sensation; but suddenly treetops came into view, and the Cossack let out a cry of alarm:

"We're sinking!" he exclaimed.

Hal laughed.

"Just coming down to get a look about," he replied. "Now, if you will look over at the earth a few moments, you will soon overcome your uneasiness."

Alexis, taking a long breath, did so; and he continued to peer over the side, even after Hal, touching the elevating lever, sent the plane high in the air again.

Darkness fell and still the 'plane sped on. Then, so suddenly that they seemed to spring up from nowhere, the swiftly moving aëroplane was surrounded on all sides—as it seemed to the voyagers—by a score of hostile aircraft, while shots rang out from several sides.

Hal acted promptly, as had always been his wont. He allowed the 'plane to drop a good quarter of a mile with a sudden lurch, and then righting it, darted forward again. For a moment they had shaken off the foe, but the latter was not long in finding them. Searchlights flashed in the sky, seeking out the prey.

By a series of clever maneuvers, Hal succeeded in evading the hostile craft during the long hours of the night, turning first this way and then that, rising and falling. But with the first gray of dawn, it became plain to both boys that escape was practically impossible. Looking down Hal saw water below him, and at the same moment the hostile air fleet ten 'planes strong, swooped down on them.

Chester's rifle cracked, as did that of Alexis. Bullets flew about all three occupants of the machine, and then the craft, struck in a vital spot, staggered. The 'plane began to sink slowly. In vain did Hal try to check the descent. The machine, still heading slightly toward the north, glided toward the water below.

Suddenly Hal made out something below besides water. It was land. The lad breathed easier, for it was plain, that at the rate at which the craft was sinking, it could clear the water by a good quarter of a mile, beyond which the lad could see a sandy coast.

"It must be the coast of Sweden or Denmark," he said to himself, "in which event we are safe, for it is neutral ground."

The Germans, realizing that their foe was sinking, did not waste another shot on it, but swarmed after. Now the craft was close to the water. Gently it skimmed over it, across a short stretch of sand, and then settled slowly to the ground.

Hal and Chester glanced about. There was no one in sight on the sandy beach and the Germans were coming right after them.

"Even though this be Sweden," said Hal, "unless Swedish troops come to our aid, the Germans are likely to violate the neutrality of the country and take us anyhow."

"Not without a fight," declared Alexis. "Let me get my feet on the ground again, and I will show you such a fight as you never saw. On the ground I can fight."

Now the 'plane was but a few scant yards from the earth. It grounded with a shock.

CHAPTER XXIX

THE DEATH OF A TITAN

Quickly the three leaped out. In spite of the Germans hovering overhead, Hal examined the 'plane.

"Great Scott!" he exclaimed, after a quick, though careful, inspection. "I can fix this thing in five minutes."

Now the German machines came to the ground a short distance away. From each craft leaped three men, who dashed toward the three friends.

Alexis turned to Hal and Chester.

"Do you," he said calmly, "fix up the airship. I will meet these fellows!"

Before either lad could reply, he had hurled himself upon the foe.

For some reason, probably because they did not wish to attract the attention of the Swedish authorities by the sounds of a struggle, the Germans, at first, drew no firearms. Perceiving but one form rushing toward them, they advanced to meet him confidently. Plainly they considered it the wild dash of a madman.

Hal and Chester turned their attention to the aëroplane, and while Alexis fought against overwhelming numbers, they overhauled it carefully.

Right into the midst of his foes rushed the giant. Such a superb attack was never seen before–such a mad wild dash as he took the enemy by surprise and hurled them back–all of them–back against the airships that stood on the sands.

As the huge Cossack rushed forward, his sword flashed above his head. His revolver he gripped tightly by the barrel. A fighting fire darted from his eye, and his thin lips were bared in a slight smile.

If ever a man felt the joy of battle it was he. He heeded not the number of his adversaries nor the steel that flashed forth against him. Slashing, cutting, parrying, thrusting, he hurled himself in upon them. They were carried back by the very fierceness of his attack. They gave way before him, parting to retreat around one of the aircraft. With one swift sweep of his foot, Alexis tore a ragged hole in the bottom of the first craft; and at the same instant two men fell beneath his slashing blows.

They could not stand before him–their very numbers were against them as the giant pressed ever forward. Now a man dropped to the ground and seized the giant by the left leg, thinking to drag him down. Alexis drove his right boot into the man's face, and at the same moment, by a quick backhanded sweep of his sword, cut down a man who would have sprung upon his back.

His revolver rose and fell, once, twice, three times, and beneath these crushing blows more Germans went down. But Alexis did not escape unscathed. A sword thrust had pierced his chest, not deeply, but the blood streamed forth. There was a gaping wound in his cheek; his clothing was pierced in a dozen places.

But in spite of this he pressed on. He thought only of advance, never of retreat; and as he hurled his gigantic body, time after time, upon the overwhelming number of his foes, they gave back in consternation and astonishment.

Ten men lay dead upon the ground, their skulls battered by fierce blows of the revolver, or pierced through and through by the great sword.

And now Hal and Chester, the aëroplane once more ready for flight, dashed forward to the rescue with loud cries.

They ranged themselves alongside the fighting Cossack. He greeted them with a half-smile; he had no time for more. Three men threw themselves upon him. One he hurled from him with a stroke of his mighty leg, another felt the weight of his revolver butt and the third fell back with a sword wound in his chest.

Unmindful of his own danger, the giant turned to the aid of Chester, who, at that moment was at the mercy of an enemy's sword. A mighty stroke of the massive arm and the German lay dead on the ground.

The Germans, having had the worst of this encounter with a single foe, stood back and drew their revolvers. Quickly Alexis reversed his own weapon and fired. There was one enemy less. A bullet struck him in the chest. He staggered, but recovered, and again fired at his foes.

The revolvers of the two lads were also spitting fire. A bullet grazed Hal's head and he toppled over. He was up in a moment, however, fighting more fiercely than before. Chester felt a stinging sensation in his right arm. Quickly he transferred his weapon to his left hand, and it continued to send out its deadly missiles.

But this unequal contest could not last. It must be ended.

Alexis, wounded in a score of places, his giant body hacked and hewn, hurled himself forward in one last desperate attack. Germans quailed before the very fury of his face; they tumbled here and there beneath his sword, or sweeping blows of his now empty revolver. A bullet struck the giant in the throat. He dropped his revolver and clapped his hand to the wound. Another struck him in the shoulder. He sprang forward, struck down another of the enemy, then staggered back.

And at that moment there came the sound of tramping footsteps on the sand. Turning quickly Hal and Chester perceived approaching rapidly a body of Swedish troops. The Germans saw them at the same instant. They were still a mile away across the sands, but the Germans had no mind to be caught and interned. Quickly they leaped for their aircraft, all except those who remained upon the sands, their faces turned upward or buried therein.

Hal and Chester each seized Alexis by an arm and dragged him back toward their own aëroplane, now righted and waiting only the touch that would send it into the air. The giant Cossack staggered along, but it was plain to both lads that he was about to collapse.

"Come, come, Alexis!" cried Hal, trying to urge him on. "Only a few more steps and we will be all right."

To the very side of the craft they carried him; but here, shaking himself free of their detaining hands, he suddenly fell, face forward, upon the ground. Quickly the two lads bent over him, and succeeded in turning him on his back.

His voice came in faint gasps. The boys bent near to catch what he was saying.

"Leave me here! You go on!" came his voice. "I am done for! Save yourselves!"

The lads waited to hear no more. Chester took him by the feet and Hal by the head, and with great effort succeeded in placing him within the aëroplane, stretching him out, as well as they could across two of the seats. Then Chester sprang in and Hal jumped to the wheel.

Along the beach the craft skimmed lightly, then arose from the ground. At the same instant a volley rang out from the approaching Swedish troops and the officer in command called out to surrender. The German airships, for some unaccountable reason, had not waited to resume the fight upon ascending into the air, but had made off.

Hal headed the aëroplane due westward, making for the coast of England. Alexis had lapsed into unconsciousness upon being placed in the machine, but now he stirred feebly and spoke.

"A real fight, wasn't it?" he gasped. "I told you I could do it if I were on the ground. How many was it I killed? Twenty–thirty–forty—"

He broke off and burst into a fit of coughing. Chester bent over him anxiously.

"You'll be all right in a day or two, old man," he said gently.

Alexis smiled feebly.

"Don't try to fool me," he said. "I am a man. I know when death is near and I am not afraid to face it."

Both lads realized that their giant Cossack friend was near his end, but there was nothing they could do for him. Chester bound up the wounds as well as he could, stopping the flow of blood, but that was all.

As the aëroplane flew over the sea toward the coast of England, the dying man continued to talk. Now he sat up in the craft and gazed down over the side.

"I had always thought," he said slowly, "that I should end my days in my own land. As it is I shall not end them in any land at all; but in the air. It is strange."

Hal slowed the aëroplane down until it was barely moving and turned to Alexis.

"You are wrong," he said. "You are not going to die. In a few hours we shall be in England, where you shall have the best of medical attention."

"It is too late," replied the Cossack calmly. "I shall not live an hour."

His breath came with difficulty.

"There is one thing I should like to know," he said.

"What is it, Alexis?" asked Hal.

"Will you tell me what you meant by 'drawing the long bow'?"

Hal was silent for some moments, and then replied gravely.

"When a man boasts of things he has never done, in America it is called 'drawing the long bow.' I was mistaken in your case. It would be impossible for you to 'draw the long bow.' You have done too much."

"That is true," agreed Chester.

Suddenly the giant frame fell back. Hal turned as best he could while Chester leaned over him anxiously. Alexis extended a hand to each of them, which they grasped.

"This," he said, pressing their hands in a still strong grip, "is the end. I wish that I could have lived to see the outcome of this war."

"There can be but one outcome," replied Chester softly. "You may rest assured of that."

"True," said the giant, "but I would like to have seen my old home again."

The lads were silent. Finally Hal spoke.

"To think," he said, "that we are responsible for your fate; but for us you would have remained with the army and have lived to the end of the war. We are to blame."

"Sh-h-h," whispered the dying giant. The hand which held Chester's freed itself and groped in his pocket. "But for you lads," he continued, "I should never have won this."

He pulled from his pocket the Cross of St. George, pinned to his breast by the Russian emperor, and gazed at it lovingly.

"It is well worth the sacrifice," he said.

Still holding the medal his hand again sought Chester's and pressed it. His other hand still gripped Hal's.

"Good-by, boys," he said firmly. "Let the Grand Duke know."

171

The pressure upon their hands relaxed. The giant frame of Alexis Vergoff, brave man and fighter extraordinary, stiffened and lay still. He was dead.

And as the aëroplane swept over the sea to the distant coast of England Hal and Chester mourned the loss of a true and stanch friend.

Arrived in England the lads saw the body of Alexis laid to rest with fitting honors, and continued their mission to the continent, where Hal put the document entrusted to his care by the Russian Grand Duke Nicholas into the hands of Field Marshal Sir John French, commander-in-chief of the British forces on the continent.

And so we shall take leave of them for a short time. Their subsequent adventures will be found in a succeeding volume, entitled: "The Boy Allies in the Trenches; or Midst Shot and Shell Along the Aisne."

THE END